The Beggars' Ride

A Richard Jackson Book

The BEGGARS' RIDE

*To Teri —
How lovely to
meet you!*

Theresa Nelson

*2/21/'98   Many thanks!
Theresa Nelson*

ORCHARD BOOKS · NEW YORK

Permission to quote from the following songs is gratefully acknowl-
edged. "BRAIN DAMAGE," words and music by Roger Waters.
TRO—© copyright 1973 Hampshire House Publishing Corp.,
New York, NY. Used by permission. "BORN FREE" by Don Black
and John Barry, © 1966 Screen Gems-EMI Music Inc. All rights
reserved. International copyright secured. Used by permission.
"STORMY WEATHER," lyric by Ted Koehler, music by Harold Arlen.
Copyright © 1933. Renewed 1961. All rights for the extended term
of copyright administered by Fred Ahlert Music Corporation on
behalf of Ted Koehler Music Company. Harold Arlen share administered by SA Music. All rights reserved. Rights outside of the
U.S.A. controlled by Mills Music, Inc., c/o EMI Catalog Partner-
ship. "SOMETIMES I'M HAPPY" (Vincent Youmans, Irving Caesar),
© 1925 WB Music Corp., Irving Caesar Music Corp., and Mirose
Music. All rights on behalf of Irving Caesar Music Corp. administered by WB Music Corp. (renewed). All rights reserved. Used by
permission.

Orchard Books
95 Madison Avenue
New York, NY 10016

Manufactured in the United States of America
Book design by Mina Greenstein
The text of this book is set in 11 point Electra.
4   6   8   10   9   7   5   3

Library of Congress Cataloging-in-Publication Data
Nelson, Theresa, date.
The beggars' ride / by Theresa Nelson.
p.   cm. "A Richard Jackson book"—Half t.p.
Summary: Twelve-year-old Clare flees an unhappy home life and
tries to survive on the streets of Atlantic City with a small gang of
homeless kids, each of whom has his own secret reason for dis-
trusting society.
ISBN 0-531-05896-4.   ISBN 0-531-08496-5 (lib. bdg.)
[1. Runaways—Fiction. 2. Homeless
persons—Fiction. 3. Atlantic City (N.J.)—
Fiction. 4. Child molesting—Fiction.]
I. Title. PZ7.N4377Be 1992 [Fic]—dc20 90-52515

For my sons,
MICHAEL, BRIAN, and ERROL COONEY—
remembering our summer on the boardwalk

☐

"It's gettin' kind of *dangerous* out there."
—James L. (age sixteen)

from "Wild in the Streets" by Eliott Currie,
for the *Los Angeles Times Magazine*, Dec. 15, 1991

1

THERE SHOULD have been thunder.

The lightning made her restless, and so Clare Frances Caldwell lay awake all that last night in Nashville, waiting for the sound that was sure to follow. Counting her fingers, over and over: three Mississippi, four Mississippi; five for each mile away, wasn't it? Or was it only two? Not that it mattered; must have been heat lightning, after all, because the thunder never came. And finally along about daybreak she gave up listening for it and decided to cut her hair.

The job took a while because she couldn't find the regular scissors without turning on the light in Mama's room, which at that hour would have caused them both no end of grief, and so she had to make do with the small blunt-edged pair she had used in kindergarten. These were dull and eight-years rusty; also she had a lot of hair, long silky masses of it that hung below her shoulder blades, not blond, exactly, but not really brown either. "Color of caramel candy," Mama's new boyfriend had said admiringly, which only made Clare all the more anxious to be rid of it.

For nearly an hour she stood at the sink, absorbed in her task, while the small patch of sky outside the bathroom window lightened gradually from slate to purple to milky gray—snipping, sawing really, clump by clump, until her head looked like a war zone.

A year ago—a week, even—the damage would have made her want to cry. Her hair was the only thing about her that anyone had ever called beautiful.

"Just like your Aunt Sister's," Mama would say in the old days, when she used to brush and braid it for Clare every morning before school. "Thank goodness you got *something* from my side." Meaning it was bad luck that Clare owed just about everything else—long bony frame and big ears and even the gap between her two front teeth—to her good-for-nothing daddy, Gordon D. Caldwell, who had long since skipped not just town but the entire continent: when last heard of he was working on an oil rig in the North Sea. "Yes, ma'am, you take care of this hair, and that's what people will notice. Hold still now, I'm not hurting you."

She was, though; Mama had steel in her fingers. But Clare had held still because it was never a good idea to cross Mama, and anyhow she was willing to suffer for the sake of her one and only beauty—the bulk of which now lay in tatters in the yellow plastic trash can under the sink.

Once she would have cried, for sure. But now she took a kind of grim satisfaction in her crop of ragged spikes. Its ugliness pleased her. The old Clare Frances was gone forever; here was the new, improved version, sharp as freshly broken glass. She gritted her teeth, lifted her chin, and stared down the stranger in the mirror. Then she took a deep breath and opened a bottle she had picked up the night before at the cosmetics counter in Wal-Mart, and when she was finished, the spikes were orange. "October Auburn" the label had promised, but Lady Clairol was a liar.

"It don't matter," she told her reflection. "Joey Morgan don't care what you look like. Joey Morgan would be glad to see you even if you were bald."

The thought was like the man-made air bubble at the deep end of the public pool where she had learned to swim; ducking inside it, she could breathe again.

She cleaned up the mess in the bathroom, taking care not to leave any trace of her transformation. She flushed the hair down the toilet, washed out the sink, carried the dye bottle into the kitchen, where she buried it in an old milk carton in the garbage. Back in her bedroom, she dressed hastily, putting on underwear and cutoff jeans and one of Mama's brassieres from the dirty-clothes hamper (she had to pin it in back and stuff it with toilet paper in front and even then it looked weird, but what the heck, she figured, it was better than nothing); also a webbed belt with a fake silver buckle in the shape of a rose, a black Pink Floyd T-shirt: "See You on the Dark Side of the Moon"© said the logo; and a pair of green spiked heels that she remembered at the last second, stuck away in a dusty corner of her closet. Mama had got sick of them years ago, loaned them to Clare for playing dress-up when she was a kid. They pinched a bit now, but not enough to matter. They would do.

From its hiding place under her mattress she took a dog-eared envelope, put it in her pocket, and then walked into the combination TV/living room to the cluttered coffee table where Mama's black handbag was lying half-open, spilling its contents onto the phony wood-grain finish: old wads of Kleenex and makeup and gum wrappers, keys and grocery store receipts and a couple of miniature gin bottles (empty now) that she had brought back from an airplane trip to Mobile last month—

And a worn leather wallet.

Calmly, almost as if she were watching someone else do it—someone in a movie maybe, who had nothing to do with her—Clare picked it up, counted out forty-four dollars, put the bills in her pocket. There was more, but she didn't take it; forty-four was all she had to have for her ticket, and Mama would need the rest to see her through till next payday. Clare put the wallet back now, closed the handbag, then on second thought opened it again and took out a half pack of Juicy Fruit, a tube of Tahiti Sunrise lip gloss, and—as long as she was sinning anyway—a pair of blue sunglasses with mirrored lenses.

She closed the handbag one more time, placed it back where she had found it, and crossed the room soundlessly—scarcely breathing as she passed the door to the other bedroom, where Mama lay snoring gently in the crook of her lover's arm. If she woke, if she saw Clare now, that would be the end of everything. "Good God Almighty, girl!" she would holler. "What's going on here? What have you *done* to yourself?" And if last night's liquor hadn't worn off yet, she would do more than holler.

But Mama wasn't going to see her.

Not ever again.

2

ATLANTIC CITY looked faintly blue. Not just the ocean and the sky but the whole island—the sand was blue and so were the sea gulls, and up here above the crowded beach the boardwalk was blue, too: flashy blue casinos and trashy blue arcades, hairy-legged tourists in blue Bermuda shorts, brushing past benches where old people sat in the hazy blue sunshine, feeding pigeons. Even the pigeons were blue, seen through the lenses of the mirrored sunglasses.

Seemed like another planet entirely.

Lord, her feet were killing her. Clare paused for a moment to get her bearings, plopped down on an empty bench, and took off the green heels that had seemed like such a good idea, half a dozen blisters ago. She wiggled her toes to get the blood back in them, took the battered envelope from her pocket, and looked for the thousandth time at the return address on the back—

J. T. Morgan
c/o Atlantic Jack's . . .

He would be there. He had to be. She'd come such a long way already—fifteen hours on three different Greyhounds yesterday, a smattering of sleep snatched last night on a station bench in Richmond, Virginia, then up before dawn this morning for the final leg of the journey through Washington, D.C., and Baltimore and Philadelphia. And that wasn't even counting the walk from the depot here, looking over her shoulder the whole time, expecting every minute to see Mama and her boyfriend following her, trying to make her come back.

As if they could.

A pigeon with dirty blue feet and a shiny blue neck pecked at a half-eaten pretzel near her big toe, making her jump, then flew away with a frantic flapping of wings. Clare watched it join the sea gulls screeching and circling overhead—drawn, she figured, by the smells drifting out of a hundred fast-food joints and vendors' carts: hamburger grease and mustard and popcorn and the heavy sweetness of cotton candy. Carnival smells. Her own stomach rumbled, but she paid it no mind, forcing herself not to count the hours since she had last eaten—a box of Cracker Jacks swiped from the candy counter at the Roanoke terminal. There were some things, she told herself, more important than food.

Joey Morgan's face, for one. The way it would light up like New Year's Eve when he saw her. "Hey, kiddo!" he'd say. "What a great surprise! How long can you stay?"

"Forever," she whispered, turning the word over on her tongue as if it were a piece of chocolate. *Forever*. It tasted sharp and sweet at once, made her stomach lurch as she stuffed her feet back into the green shoes and continued down the boardwalk: past the Dip Stix IV and the Miss America Food Court and the Four Lucky Sisters From Italy Casino Arcade. Past Bally's Grand and Peanut World and the booth where a man in a straw hat was giving out fliers for the $1,000,000 Megabucks Sweepstakes: "One Pull Can Change Your Life," they announced. Just behind him was a cot where a woman who had neither arms nor legs was lying facedown, playing a portable keyboard with her tongue. Clare recognized the melody from her seventh-grade music appreciation class—

Born free, as free as the wind blows . . .

"What are you staring at?" The woman's companion was a surly young man who frowned at Clare and shook his donations box in her face. "Go on, get out of here!"

And so she moved on quickly, past a mall built to look like a ship sticking out over the water, past a towering concrete emperor with a pair of pigeons on his head, past Madame Edna's Phrenology and Psychic Counseling: PALMS, TAROT CARDS, CRYSTAL-BALL SPECIAL ONLY $4.99 WITH COUPON—until she came at last to an odd sand-colored building with peeling turquoise trim and looming stained-glass windows. An old church, maybe? Or not a church, exactly—more of a mini Arabian palace, topped with elaborate towers and turrets. ATLANTIC JACK'S, said the sign on the marquee. WORLD-FAMOUS HOT DOGS.

A hot-dog joint? What would Joey be doing in a place like this? He was a musician, for crying out loud, not a cook or a waiter. But then maybe there were apartments upstairs, or maybe they had live music at night—could be any number of explanations.

7

Clare paused at the window, checked out her reflection. She had hoped the new getup—shoes and shades and hairdo and all—would make her look older than twelve and three-quarters, fool anyone who might come across her picture on the back of some milk carton. It had made perfect sense at four in the morning, but now in broad daylight—*Lord*. She searched her pockets for a comb, came up empty-handed. Then she spit on her fingers in desperation, ran them through the orange spikes. She wished—

And then she stopped herself. *If wishes were horses, beggars would ride.* It was the only nursery rhyme Mama had ever taught her. Besides, it really didn't matter, did it? Nothing mattered, as long as she found Joey. As long as he let her stay.

"Even if you were bald," she repeated under her breath, and then she pushed open the door, and walked inside.

"I'm looking for Joey Morgan," she said, stepping up to the counter. A small dark man was standing behind it, fiddling with an odd contraption: a miniature Ferris wheel that appeared to be hooked up to the soda fountain.

"Eeeeah," he groaned as she approached. "Come on, stupid jerk machine. Why you never work right for Santiago?"

"Excuse me," said Clare.

"One minute, please," Santiago said. He gave the gadget a little whack with the flat of his hand. "Be right with you, miss. Just one minute more."

A whole minute. It seemed a lot to ask. But Clare waited as patiently as she could, her eyes adjusting slowly as they traveled around the dim little restaurant—twice as dim through the blue sunglasses.

It was early yet for the lunch crowd; only a handful of customers were scattered around the dozen or so tables. Atlantic Jack's was a hodgepodge of a place, filled with old-timey billboards for Burma-Shave and Dr. Daily's Hair Restorer and Laurel and Hardy in *Sons of the Desert*. On one wall a ledge had been built for an elaborate train set; just then the engine was chugging past a large photograph of a man wearing a beard of bees. A hand-carved motto was nailed beneath it: HE IS ONLY RICH, WHO OWNS THE DAY.—*Ralph Waldo Emerson.* Just opposite was a beauty of a jukebox with bubble lights traveling around its curved rim and "Star Dust"—a favorite of Joey's—pouring out of it. And above all this, suspended by invisible wires hanging from the ceiling, were airplanes: hundreds of model airplanes—the old-fashioned sort with double wings, mostly—red ones with black crosses, yellow with blue circles, silver with green, and on and on, until Clare felt dizzy with looking at them and turned her eyes back to Santiago, who had finally persuaded the soda wheel to spin around.

"Yes!" he cried as it whirred to life, lifting a frosted glass in one of its elf-sized seats. Then "No!" as two spigots suddenly opened at once, missing the glass entirely. "Eeeeeah, A.J.! Look here what your stupid jerk machine is doing to me now!" Santiago jumped to mop up the mess with a towel, all the while shaking his fist at the mechanical monster.

Clare tried again. "Excuse me. . . ."

"Sorry, miss. I should throw this machine in the junk pile maybe, then I take your order."

"I don't want to order. I'm looking for Joey Morgan. For Mr. Joseph Morgan, I mean."

Santiago's head jerked up. He looked sharply at Clare, then pulled a plug that brought the wheel clanking to a halt. "For who, you say?"

"Mr. Joseph T. Morgan. Joseph Thomas Morgan. This is the address he sent." She held out the envelope.

Santiago took one look at it, then shook his head and waved it away. "No Joe Morgan here, miss. You go on, please. Wrong address."

"This is Atlantic Jack's, isn't it?"

"Yes, miss, but nobody is here by that name. You go away, please."

"I can't go away. I have to see Joey Morgan." Panic was rising in Clare's throat, making her voice sound shrill. What was wrong with this guy, anyhow?

"Please, miss, you want a nice hot dog? Santiago will fix you up real good, no charge, then you go."

"I don't want a hot dog. What's the matter? Why are you whispering?"

"What's the trouble, Santiago?"

The quiet voice was somehow more startling than a shout would have been. Clare swung around to see an old man approaching the counter from a door off to the side of the kitchen. A tall, skinny fellow, balding on top, with a shaggy gray caterpillar of a mustache crawling along his upper lip. He was smiling a little, more with his eyes than his mouth. Blue eyes, one very clear and light, the other an odd, cloudy sort of blue.

"Nothing, A.J." Santiago glanced nervously from his boss to Clare, then back again. "Wrong address, that's all."

"I'm looking for Joey Morgan," Clare said in a rush, thrusting the envelope toward the old man—A.J., Santiago had called him; Atlantic Jack himself, then? "This is the address he sent me."

At the mention of Joey's name, the smile faded and the mismatched eyes opened wide. A.J. stared for a moment, then took the envelope and held it at arm's length, studying it. Next he took out a pair of black-rimmed glasses from his shirt pocket and put them on. One of the stems was missing, so he had to hold them in place on his nose as he peered at the envelope for what seemed to Clare like a very long time. His eyebrows drew together, and three deep creases appeared on his forehead. *Why doesn't he say anything?* Clare wondered. *Is he deaf?*

"Joey Morgan," she repeated in a louder voice. "I said I'm looking for Joe—"

"Yes, miss." The old man was speaking so softly now that Clare could scarcely hear him. He was still staring at the slapdash scrawl on the back of the envelope. "I'm sorry, Miss"—he turned it over—"Miss Caldwell. Joseph Morgan hasn't lived here in some time."

Clare's heart lurched. "But I have to find him. Do you know where he is?" Maybe it wasn't such a big deal. He had moved to a better place, that was all. Of course Joey Morgan could do better than a hot-dog joint. "Didn't he leave a—" She hesitated. What did you call those things?

"A forwarding address?" The old man shook his head, handed back the envelope. "I'm sorry. He said that he would, once he got settled out West, but that was before last Christmas and—"

"West? How far west?"

A.J. didn't answer right away. He took off the glasses, folded the one stem, then stood looking at them as if they

11

puzzled him some way. "California," he said quietly after a moment—more to his spectacles, it appeared, than to Clare. "That's where he said he was headed."

California! On the other side of the country—clear across the continent! California! It took Clare's breath away, that one word. Made her feel as if the earth were tilting beneath her feet. Or maybe she was just hungry; it had been a while since those Cracker Jacks. . . .

"Are you all right, miss?" A.J. put a hand under her elbow to steady her, but at his touch she stiffened, drew back. She leaned against a stool for support until the world stopped swaying so.

"I'm fine."

"Santiago, maybe the young lady would like something cold to drink."

Santiago, who was still watching Clare with his sharp dark eyes, nodded now and started to give the soda wheel another spin. But Clare shook her head. Her throat felt as if it had swollen shut; she didn't believe she could swallow a drop. "No," she said, louder than she had to. "No, thank you."

There was a moment's awkward silence. Then A.J. coughed. "Miss Caldwell, I don't mean to pry, but are you a—a relative of Joseph's?"

Clare hesitated. Was there such a thing as an ex-step-father? Not that her claim on Joey was even as official as that; he and Mama had never married, though they had been together for nearly five years, off and on. Not that it mattered anymore. "No," she said. "Just a—no." She turned away, started to move toward the door.

"Miss Caldwell."

Clare turned around.

"There have been a number of letters that have come for Joseph during the past year. I suppose I should have returned them, but I kept expecting that he would send me his new address, and so—"

Clare felt the blood rush to her face. Her letters—

Dear Joey, please come back, its worse than before. . . . Please Joey I know your busy but you don't know what its like with this new guy here. . . . Lissen if you can't get away its ok I could come to you anytime you say. . . . I wouldn't be any trouble, I could cook for you remember like I use to, I can still fry chicken real good, love Clare. . . .

The thought of them sickened her now. Was this old man laughing at her? "You *read* them?"

"No, no, certainly not." A.J. seemed dismayed at the suggestion. "But I recognized your name from the envelopes, you see, and I just thought—possibly—you might want them back?" He was tripping over his words, as if they stood in his way somehow.

Clare nodded, not trusting her voice.

"Just a moment." A.J. crossed the room, disappeared through a door marked No Admittance, then reappeared a few moments later, carrying a stack of letters—about ten deep, tied with a red rubber band. He handed them to her.

"Thanks," she muttered. Once more she turned to go; once more the old man called her back.

"Miss Caldwell."

This time Clare stopped without turning around.

"I'm sorry I couldn't help you."

Clare shrugged. Probably she should have said something—"That's all right," or "Sorry to trouble you," or "Thank you for your time," or some junk like that—but her throat was still thick and aching, and there was no way

13

she was going to stand here sniveling in front of some old guy she didn't know from Adam.

He was still speaking. "I hope you didn't come all this way for . . ." He hesitated, then went on, "Are you here with your family?"

Alarm bells went off in Clare's head. He was asking far too many questions. "Uh, sure," she stammered, her mind racing. "We're here on—on vacation, visiting my—my grandmother."

"I see. . . . Well, if you'd like to leave her address, then I could contact you if there's any word."

"No—no, thanks. It don't matter." Clare was moving toward the door again. This old guy knew too much already. What if he had lied, if he had read the letters, after all? If while he was in the other room he had stopped at the phone and called the police, and now he was stalling, trying to get her to hang around until they got here? Until they locked her up or sent her to some reformatory or, even worse, tried to make her go back—

"Miss Caldwell?"

But Clare was already out the door, moving quickly down the boardwalk, holding tightly to the packet of letters, her face still hot with the shame of them. She hurried to leave behind the weird little hot-dog palace, the crowded shops and casinos and popcorn vendors, the ugly blue motel with the starfish in its windows and the postage stamp of a pool where big-bellied men and freckled women and shriek-ing children clustered, as if they didn't have sense enough to know they were two minutes from a whole ocean. She walked faster, faster, down a creaky set of wooden steps that took her onto the beach, into the sand—hot, dry sand that poured into the green spiked heels and made it impossible to walk. And so she took them off, carried them; the sand was so hot then it burned her feet, but she was almost glad because it was the kind of pain she could manage, easier to bear than the pain in her head, her throat: *California, for pete's sake, Cali-freaking-fornia.*

And now she was running, as if she were being chased, though she didn't know for sure if anyone was chasing her, running across the searing sand, dodging tourists, scattering seabirds, running until she found an open space all her own at the edge of the water, where she hurled the packet of letters as far as she could—*Dear Joey, please Joey, I just want to be with you Joey*—out into the Atlantic Ocean, out past the big breakers and a pair of startled pelicans and a lone girl swimmer with a bathing cap trimmed in pink rubber flowers, out into a stretch of calm green water, where they disappeared without even much of a splash.

3

THAT NIGHT she slept in the belly of a whale, a kid-sized model cast in concrete—or stucco or plaster or whatever the heck they make those things out of. It was in a playground just off the boardwalk, away from the glittering carnival lights of the casinos, down around Ventnor, where there were mostly rooming houses and small family businesses. The playground was only a fair-sized stretch of muddy sand, really, filled with the usual swings and slides and a menagerie of violently colored sea creatures: a bright yellow sea horse, a blue-and-red spotted octopus, a poison green sea lion balancing a magenta ball on its nose. And this whale, which was purple with a wide pink grin.

Clare climbed in through the grin just after midnight, just as a pale half-moon was rising out over the ocean. An even paler ring encircled it like a fuzzy halo.

"Ring around the moon means the fairies will be dancing," Joey Morgan had told her once.

"Is that true?" she asked, looking where he pointed out the kitchen window. She was just a little kid back then, no more than five or six.

Joey had laughed and put his arms around her, his cheek next to hers. "Could be," he whispered. "I don't know anyone who can prove it's not."

Mama, chopping onions at the table, had sniffed. "Ring like that means it'll rain tomorrow, that's all," she said. And it had.

Now Clare scrunched back as far as she could, into the tail, then pillowed her head on her arm, lying sideways. This whale wasn't half-bad, compared to the beds she had tried earlier: the first, a pile of rotting timber under the boardwalk, where she had hunkered until a barking dog had frightened her away; the second, an abandoned shell of a car on a semideserted side street behind Trop World. That had seemed okay until a bleary-eyed man wandered over, reached through the smashed rear window, and unlocked the back door. Clare had fled before he got any closer. Maybe he was just a harmless drunk, but she wasn't about to hang around and find out for sure.

No, the whale wasn't bad at all. A little damp maybe, a touch on the smelly side, but at least she had a roof over her head, that was the main thing. Couldn't anybody see her without her seeing them first—no stumbling winos or meddling policemen or beach patrol, asking questions.

If only it weren't so dark. She hated the dark. Still, it could have been worse. Fairies or no, half a moon was better than none.

She closed her eyes, tried to picture California—oranges growing in the middle of winter, palm trees and movie stars, a big red ball of a sun sinking into the ocean. . . . Listen,

listen, you could hear it, even—the rush of the wind, the crash of the waves. *No, wait—this is the wrong ocean, ain't it?* She was already half-asleep; her mind was playing tricks, jumbling geography. But the oceans ran together, didn't they? If you looked on a globe, all the blue was con- nected. . . . Maybe she should write another letter, put this one in a bottle before she threw it into the water. Let it drift away on the current, float south to the Gulf of Mexico. Then through that canal they had down there, straight on out to the Pacific, until it washed ashore, finally, on the very beach where Joey Morgan might just happen to be strolling some balmy California afternoon. "What's this?" he'd ask himself, picking it up. "Dear Joey, I'm living in a whale in New Jersey, come soon, love Clare."

"Well, I'll be!" he'd say out loud. "Wait right there, kiddo. Wait up, I'm coming!"

Clare jerked awake, sat up so suddenly she bumped her head on the whale's rib cage. This was no dream; that wasn't Joey's voice. Someone was out there, shouting, running in the playground.

"Yo, Cowboy! D'jya see the look on that fat guy's face? Man, I thought he's gonna bust a gut when he saw you gone!"

"Hee, hee, hee!"

"Looked just like one of them, what you call 'em, blow- fish? Listen to old Shoe laugh. He knows what I mean!"

"Hee, hee, hee!"

"Cool it, you guys. We ain't been nowhere tonight— got that? Got that, everybody?"

"Nowhere but here, Little Dog, hangin' on the monkey bars. Don't I know?"

Kids, thought Clare, breathing a little easier. *Just a*

bunch of stupid kids. She flattened herself against the inside of the whale's left cheek, peered out the corner of its smile. She could see them clearly in the moonlight: four—no, five. One big girl—a tough-looking frizzed-out blond with bracelets crowding one another on her arms and silver earrings dangling from every one of the half-dozen holes she seemed to have poked in each ear—the rest a sorry collection of guys who could have been anywhere from twelve to twenty. One of the younger ones wore a black patch over his left eye, but it was apparently just for show; he flipped it up over his eyebrow while he climbed to the top of the jungle gym and tickled a skinny little squirt with oddly mottled skin. He was hanging by his knees, upside down.

"Hee, hee, hee!"

"Look at Shoe—his eyes bulging outa his head, just like the blowfish man!"

"Leave him alone, Racer. You guys come down from there before somebody sees you. What are you, babies?" A fat kid was speaking now. He sat on one of the octopus's tentacles, holding a flashlight with one hand, scribbling with the other in a notebook he had propped up in his lap.

"Let 'em stay up there, L.D. More for us that way," said the blond. She was setting out food on a picnic table— french fries, judging from the smell. It brought water to Clare's mouth, tears to her eyes, practically. She had had too much on her mind today to worry about food; only now did she remember how hungry she was.

"What?" The patch-eyed kid—Racer?—started to scramble down, giving his buddy one last poke in the ribs. "Hear that, Shoe? They wanta eat my share!"

The skinny kid swung himself upright and attempted to follow, but Racer blocked his way, kept up his teasing:

19

"Naw, baby boy, you gonna get fat as Little Dog if you don't watch out. Then whatchoo gonna do? Thought for a minute there tonight you was stuck in that little window, gonna hafta stay there till the blue boys come and pull you out."

"That's enough, Racer." The kid with the notebook was speaking again. "Didn't I already tell you to cool it?"

"Shoot, man." Racer plopped himself down on the table, started to stuff french fries in his mouth. "Ain't nobody listenin'."

"You sure of that?"

A new voice this time, deeper than the others. Clare couldn't see the speaker; he was just out of her line of vision. But something about the way he said that handful of words brought sweat to her palms.

"Sure I'm sure."

"Check it out anyway."

Clare pressed back into the creature's tail. Had he spotted her?

"What's the matter, Cowboy?" It was the girl speaking now. "Did you see—" She broke off there, as if she had been hushed. And then for an agonizing minute no one spoke, and if they were moving, they moved so quietly that Clare couldn't hear them, though she could imagine them clearly enough: snooping in corners, peering behind bushes, creeps creeping around the playground, looking for *her*. Suddenly she was five years old again, playing at hide-and-go-seek, heart thudding painfully in her chest. *Well, let them look*, she told herself. *You've got as much right to be here as they do.* She thought about running but decided against it. They were sure to see her then; better to stand her ground, hang tough. Still, her breathing sounded much too loud in her own ears, and she had to cross her legs to keep from squirming; hide-and-go-seek always did make her want to go to the bathroom—

"Well, looky here. This whale has swallowed hisself a fish!"

Racer was squatting by the whale's mouth, grinning at Clare. The pirate's patch was still flipped up over his left eyebrow. "Whatchoo doin' in there, Fish? Time you was swimmin' home to Mama, ain't it?"

Clare sat up straight, folded her arms across her chest. "None of your business," she muttered.

"Happen it is. Happen you got your bony behind parked in my bedroom, Fishy."

"Ain't yours," Clare growled. "Public property, looks like to me. I was here first."

"Naw, man, you must be new in town, don't know nothin' yet, that's all. Boardwalk's our territory, bottom to top. Whales included."

"Find something, Racer?"

At first Clare saw only his legs, blue-jeaned, longer than hers. And his sneakers—black high tops with silver wings on the sides. New looking, neatly laced.

"Some girl in my spot, Cowboy. Says she was here first. I told her she'd have to get out."

Now Cowboy was squatting beside the first kid, looking in at Clare. The moonlight came from behind him, framing him, so it was hard to see much more than his outline: curly black hair, an athlete's build—that much she could make out. That and his eyes, which were dark but seemed to hold a peculiar light of their own. They cut straight through the gloom, set a cold line of perspiration trickling down the inside of her left arm.

He said nothing for a moment, just kept his eyes fixed on Clare's while the other kids gathered around him, buzzing.

"What you gonna do with her, Cowboy?"

"She can't stay."

"Can't just let her go, can we? How much did she hear?"

"What if she told the cops?"

"She ain't gonna tell nobody nothin'." It was the girl who spoke up loudest. She knelt beside Cowboy, her thigh pressed possessively against his. "She ain't gonna say a word. Knows I'll get her if she tries."

Clare sniffed. "Think I'm scared of *you?*"

The girl scowled. "You oughta be." She started to climb into the whale, but Cowboy held her back. "Cool it, Thimble," he said quietly.

"But you heard her—"

"I said cool it." Cowboy's voice was still low, but there was something about it that shut everybody up, turned Clare's insides to water. *Good grief,* she thought, *he's got us all waiting for his permission to breathe.* Which irritated her somehow. She lifted her chin defiantly, looked him in the eye, tried to think of something wonderful to say. And couldn't.

He was silent for a moment more, studying her. Then, "You're not from around here, are you?"

Clare hesitated, then shook her head. That much seemed safe to admit. Besides, there wasn't much point in lying; her accent gave her away anyhow. No way she could imitate the flat A's and peculiar R's she had heard coming out of these New Jersey mouths.

"Where, then?"

Clare shrugged.

The girl—Thimble?—leaned in threateningly. "Cowboy asked you a question."

But he held up a hand, and she fell silent again. There was no sound but the wind blowing in from the sea, the distant hum of traffic from beyond the darkened houses. Cowboy picked up a handful of sand, let it run through his fingers. "How long have you been running?"

"Who said I was running?"

Cowboy put his head to one side, glanced at the dirty pink walls of the whale's underbelly. He made a faint whistling sound—something between a sigh and a chuckle. "You trying to tell me you're not?"

Clare followed his eyes, saw it was useless to pretend. She shrugged again. "A while," she said. Was it really only two days? Felt like a year at least.

Thimble sneered. "Green as grass."

Cowboy ignored her, kept looking at Clare. "You know how to keep quiet?"

"If I want to."

Once more Thimble started to move in threateningly; once more Cowboy held her back. He was still watching Clare—*observing* was the word that came to her mind—as if he were looking through a microscope at one of those odd specimens she had seen in science class: some hairy little one-celled guy, swimming in a drop of pond scum.

At last he nodded. "Okay, then," he said.

"*Okay?*" Thimble cried.

"Okay *what?*" Racer objected. "Ain't you gonna tell her to get outa my whale?"

"Like she said, she was here first. Tonight anyway. You and Shoe can bunk with Little Dog."

23

"Aww, man, not with the Dog! He snores!"

"You heard me." Cowboy looked at the fat kid. "Go on, L.D., take care of these guys, will you? Tuck 'em in, tell 'em a bedtime story."

Little Dog looked up from his notebook, grinned. "No sweat, Cowboy."

"Aww, man . . ."

The group broke up then, disappeared one by one into the mouths of the other sea creatures, leaving Clare alone. For a while she could hear voices coming from the direction of the sea lion, punctuated now and again by a burst of high-pitched laughter—Shoe again, she guessed: "Hee, hee, hee!" Then silence.

Had she won, then? Passed some kind of test? And even if she had, was it a test worth passing?

But she was too tired to figure it out tonight, much too tired, though she doubted that she'd ever get back to sleep now, what with her heart still pounding in her chest, throbbing in her ears. *Sleep*, she told herself, forcing her eyelids shut, burying her head in the crook of her arm. *Don't try to think. Got to get some rest, that's all. . . .*

"Hey, kid."

Clare's eyes flew open again, but this time when she sat up she took care not to bang her head. It was the big girl, the one they had called Thimble, squatting at the entrance, holding out a half-finished bag of french fries. Cold by now, surely, but Clare could still smell them. She steeled herself against the impulse to grab them, shove the lot in her mouth, bag and all.

"No, thanks."

"Go on, take 'em. Wasn't my idea." Thimble was scowling again. It was Cowboy who had sent her, then. "Don't mean he likes you," she added scornfully. "They were left over, that's all."

"I'm not hungry."

The scowl deepened. "Go on, take 'em. Whaddya think—I poisoned 'em?"

"I told you before, I ain't scared of you."

Now it was Thimble's turn to shrug. "Suit yourself. You don't want 'em"—she threw the bag down in the sand—"leave 'em for the rats."

"Rats?" The word escaped before Clare had a chance to catch it.

Thimble looked pleased with herself. "You'll get used to 'em," she said. "They're all over the island, big as squirrels, some. We think of them as pets." She smiled. Or maybe not *smiled*, exactly; showed her teeth was more like it. Clare was happy to see they weren't all that good.

Thimble rose, turned to go. Then she changed her mind and bent down once more, bracelets clicking menacingly, earrings dangling. They glinted silver in the moonlight; for the first time Clare noticed their resemblance to knives. "It's just for tonight, kid, you got that? After tonight, you're gone."

4

CLARE WOKE to the sound of rain falling steadily on the whale's back. *Ring around the moon—right again, Mama.* There was grit in her mouth, her hair; she felt stiff all over, sticky. But at least some of the goo had left her brain; at least the heavy weight of fatigue behind her eyes had lifted a little.

The french-fries bag lay crumpled in the sand beside her. She had eaten them once Thimble had left. Not that she had bought that garbage about the rats; it was just that in the end her pride was no match for the gnawing in her stomach. What did it matter anyhow? she had reasoned. It wasn't as if she had to prove anything to this bunch of hoods. With any luck, she'd never see them again.

She lay still for a while. It was fairly light out, but no little kids would be coming here to play in this weather. For now she was safe. The whale seemed almost cozy, compared to the world outside. Even now, with the rain leaking in from the corner of its grin, there was something comforting about the whale, something reassuringly dopey that made her feel four again, when everything was decided for her and real trouble was still distant, somebody else's nightmare. She tried to think only of this moment, to enjoy its peace. "One day at a time," Joey Morgan used to say.

She could hear him still, trying to explain when she'd asked why he and Mama didn't go ahead and get married.

"One day at a time, kiddo—that's all I can answer for. I stay because I want to, you see, not because some piece of paper says I have to." He had grinned then, like a little kid caught in some mischief, and magically pulled a quarter from behind her ear. "Quickest way to get rid of some people is to tell them they can't leave," he said, flipping it to her with a wink.

Clare had held her tongue after that, fearing she might lose him by a careless word.

But in the end it hadn't really mattered, had it?

Well, what had she expected? She should have known better than to trust a musician. A saxophone player in Nashville, for crying out loud—oil on water, jazz in the town where country was king. He belonged in New Orleans or Memphis—had actually been on his way from one to the other, the way he told it, just passing through town one night when he stopped to catch an old drummer friend's set at a little dive on Division Street. Jessie James and the Outlaws—that was the name of the band.

Mama's band. (She was really Jessica Marie Blalock at the time—having long since shed Clare's real daddy's name—but where was the music in that?) Mama had been wearing her prettiest red dress for the show. She was a knockout in just about any color, but red was her best. "I'm a winter," she had explained to Clare one time after she had her color chart done at JCPenney. "And you're a—well, it's kind of hard to say, isn't it? Sort of a cross between fall and summer—a fummer, maybe."

But Mama had been looking flat-out gorgeous that night, and singing like a regular angel from heaven. "Stormy Weather"—that was the number that got Joey's attention. Not one of your regular country tunes but a golden oldie she included in her act sometimes when she wanted to come on like an old-timey torch singer:

> Don't know why—
> There's no sun up in the sky . . .

And it must have really worked, because Joey hung around for the second set, and then the third, and then one thing had led to another, and before long he had put aside his sax for a country keyboard—he could handle just about any instrument, really, though sax would always be his first love. And then he was playing with the Outlaws, nights, and staying over at the apartment the rest of the time, until Clare could scarcely imagine her life without him. It was really something, the way he brightened the whole place, filling it with his jokes and songs and easy laughter—

On the good days, anyway. Mostly there were good days, when Joey was there. And even on the bad ones, when Jessie started drinking and picking at him for no good reason, just looking for trouble, even then he was never mean. He just wouldn't talk, was all. He would stare at the tube for hours on end and smoke one cigarette after another, or disappear altogether for days at a time.

Jessie would go crazy then. She would bang doors and

throw things and swear up one side and down the other that this was it, she wasn't putting up with this trash from anybody, no sirree, not one second longer.

The last of those times, Joey had been gone for a week when Clare was walking home from school one afternoon and heard the wail of a saxophone coming from the park. She followed the sound and found Joey in the center of the run-down band shell, playing for the local residents: ragged old men who smelled of booze and ammonia and Crazy Hilda, who was known to eat the bread that children threw for the ducks in the pond. This was the audience that was listening, spellbound, to Joey's music, to the sad/sweet voice he coaxed out of his horn. And when the last note had lingered and died, the old men had applauded and yelled "Bravo!" and Hilda, with tears streaming down her face, had climbed onto the stage and flung her arms around Joey, sax and all. And he hadn't shrunk back. He had smiled and patted her filthy back and then picked a sprig of jasmine from the broken-down trellis; he was fastening it in her wild white hair when he spotted Clare. And then he had said good-bye to Hilda and the others and joined her, and the two of them had walked home together, talking easily of one thing and another, just as if he had never been gone at all.

Clare thought it would be like it always was—that Mama would take him back once more. But this time was different. This time Mama must have been fresh-drunk, was all Clare could figure (crouching in the bathroom with her hands over her ears, trying not to hear, hearing all the same). This time Mama had called him every awful name she could think of, said he was nothing but a half-rate musician hanging around because nobody else would have him. Asked why he ever bothered coming back anyhow; did he think they *needed* any part of him? No, sir, no way, no, thank you. What they needed was a man they could count on, somebody who didn't take off every time you looked at him crooked. Next time he left, let him leave for good.

Quickest way to get rid of some people . . .

He hadn't even bothered to pack, just walked out the door with his sax and the clothes he was wearing and that was all. For weeks Clare kept hoping he'd come back. She would see his old sweater with the hole in the elbow, lying on the chair where he had dropped it, his muddy tennis shoes in the hall closet, the ballpoint pen with his tooth marks on the cap, still waiting by the phone.

But he never even called, though early on he dropped Clare a line or two. Silly postcards mostly—a penguin on roller skates, a man holding the world's largest rutabaga— dumb stuff with just a few words scrawled on the backs: *Hey, kiddo, how's it going? Everything is A-OK on the road, say how 'bout them Cardinals? Love, J.* Or *Dear Clare, did you hear the one about the home-run hitter from Maine? He's famous for his grand clams. Sorry about that, love, Joe.* And finally the note from Atlantic City: *Hello from ACNJ, kiddo, how's trix? Just got on with a new band at a club here, not bad, guess I'll stick around awhile. Hit it big on the slots last week, two cherries and a watermelon—buy yourself a pack of gum. Best, JTM.*

A five-dollar bill was folded inside the envelope. Clare didn't spend it; it was a kind of treasure, coming from his hands. But she wrote him a thank-you note, now that she had his address. And then she wrote him another letter, and another and another and another after that, though he never answered. He was awfully busy, she figured, now that he

30

had a new job and all. And then one day Mama saw her writing him again, and she went into one of her rages and gathered up all his stuff—shirts and sweaters and worn-out blue jeans and Miles Davis records, everything but the chewed-up Bic, which she overlooked—and carried it all down to the Dumpster in the parking lot. And Clare stood and watched, not crying, but with a lump of hatred growing in her chest, a hard little lump, getting harder by the minute.

Three months later Sid moved in. Sid the Slime. A doped-up steel guitarist considered by most people to be good-looking but he wasn't, not to Clare's way of thinking, with his pink-rimmed pig's eyes and curly gold hairs on the backs of his hands and fingers always slick with peanut grease. . . .

Clare closed her eyes tightly, squeezed away the pictures that paraded across her lids until nothing was left but flashes of red lightning and tiny white flecks dancing on black. From now on there was nothing behind her. All that was gone, blotted out; she would never let herself remember. Nothing ahead—that was too far away to matter. *One day at a time*—but she could do better: one minute at a time, one heartbeat. She would live moment by moment, second by second.

When she opened her eyes now, the rain had turned to drizzle. She was hungry again; she had to go to the bathroom. It was time to climb out of the whale.

There was no trace of the gang in the playground. The rain had erased even their footprints. Well, maybe she had dreamed them, after all. Whoever heard of a person named Thimble?

5

SHE HAD FOUND a public bathroom yesterday, just across the boardwalk from the convention hall where Miss America strutted her stuff every September. Clare headed there now. It stank and had no paper, but it was better than nothing, she figured; for the moment she was in too much of a hurry to be fussy.

But this time when she got there she spotted a pair of uniformed attendants sitting just inside the doors—one at the entrance, another at the exit. *Keeping watch—for what?* Clare wondered. *Drug dealers? Old ladies stealing toilet seats? Or runaways, maybe—skinny kids with spiky hair who look like they've slept in the sand.* Clare shrank back, tried to disappear into the crowd on the boardwalk. She couldn't take the chance. There was always the ocean, she supposed, if she got really desperate. Or maybe there'd be a bathroom at that ship-shaped mall.

There was, thank the Lord. Empty—that was a plus.

And fairly clean, too. No paper towels again, but at least there was soap in the dispenser. Clare washed her hands and face, then took off her shirt and cleaned up as best she could, rinsing with the strangulated little squirts of water that came out of the faucet when she punched the button on top. Drying off was trickier; the hot-air blower on the wall hadn't been installed with underarms in mind. Still, she was managing all right when the door swung open and a plump white-haired woman came in. At the sight of Clare—bare-chested and bent into a sort of S shape in front of the dryer—the woman opened her eyes wide, then glanced away in embarrassment. Clare covered herself hastily and began to murmur an apology—for what, exactly, she wasn't altogether sure—but the woman had already hustled into a stall. Clare saw her put her handbag on the floor and then pick it right back up again, as if she had thought better of it. Just an ordinary movement, but it felt like a slap in the face. *Good Lord*, Clare wondered, *she ain't afraid of me, is she?*

She worried about it all the way to the fountain counter at the Boardwalk Rexall Pharmacy, where for a little while, at least, the smell of breakfast drove all other considerations from her head. She sat down and ordered the Number Three Early-Bird Special: "Two Slices Golden Brown French Toast, Country Sausage, Fresh Juice of Your Choice, and Hot Coffee with Free Refill. All for $4.35 Plus Tax, Your Gratuity Is Appreciated."

"You sure you can pay for that, honey?" The waitress raised her penciled eyebrows.

Clare gave the woman as insulted a look as she could manage through the blue sunglasses, then fished in her pocket and held up Joey's five-dollar bill.

The waitress—Ginger, according to her name tag—took a stub of pencil from behind her ear and began scribbling on a green pad. "Sorry, honey, no offense. I have to be careful, you know? Some of these kids around here—they think they can get away with murder, you wouldn't believe it."

Clare shrugged her pardon, then folded the bill carefully and put it back inside the envelope in her pocket, touching it one last time for luck. No way she would ever spend it, not now or ever, but nobody had to know that just yet. Still, she wished her cheeks wouldn't burn so. First the old lady in the bathroom, now Ginger—did she already look like a criminal, then?

Mama would have said so, she supposed. By now she would have seen the things missing from her handbag and accused Clare of being a good-for-nothing little sneak thief, of breaking commandments like so many old dishes. Although it was peculiar; only certain commandments really got to Mama. She never seemed to worry much about False Gods or the Sabbath Day—except on the occasional Christmas or Easter—and she had certainly never lost any sleep over that adultery business. But the rules she *did* care about, she cared about with a vengeance: Not Taking the Lord's Name in Vain, for example—she was partial to that, at least where Clare was concerned. And of course Honoring Thy Mother was her all-time number-one favorite. But Thou Shall Not Steal ran it a pretty close second—maybe because of her horror of Clare turning out like her real daddy, who had already got himself a record for petty thievery when *he* split, and he was only twenty then. The slightest reminder could set Mama off about that; Clare had once been grounded for a week for wearing a pair of her earrings to school without asking.

Still, the rules had changed now, hadn't they? It was steal or starve, as close as Clare could make out; even the Pope wouldn't call you down for a thing like that. Of course she wasn't really flat-out broke yet; there was always Joey's five dollars. But she couldn't part with that, no matter if she *was* sinning.

"You kids back there—you put those magazines down unless you plan on buying them, you hear me? I told you a hundred times. . . ." Ginger was so busy yelling that she almost dropped the plate of French toast in Clare's lap. Clare pushed it back from the edge of the counter, swiveled around to see what had got the waitress so upset.

Good grief. It was the patch-eyed kid and the skinny one with the weird-looking skin and the dumb laugh—Racer and Shoe, right? Thumbing through copies of *Vogue* and *Cosmopolitan*, giggling like maniacs—at the underwear ads, most likely. Shoot, where had *they* come from? Had they followed her? Surely not; they made no sign that they had even seen her. Probably it was just a stupid coincidence. Still, Clare swiveled back around quickly, her face hotter yet. This breakfast business was tricky enough; she didn't need anybody connecting her with *that* pair.

"Think they own the boardwalk," Ginger muttered, plunking down Clare's coffee. It sloshed over the rim of the cup, making a small brown puddle in the saucer. "Steal us blind if they get the chance." She pointed a spoon at the boys. "Go on, now, you hear me? I told you before—next time I call the cops!"

"Aw, what's your problem, lady? Don't tell me—could

it be the misery of constipation?" Racer tossed something in Ginger's direction. She caught it reflexively: a box of Ex-Lax. Ginger shook it at the two as they beat it out the door, Shoe laughing fit to kill—"Hee, hee, hee!"

"Smart-mouthed kids." Ginger plopped down the maple syrup. "Somebody ought to do 'em a favor, send 'em to reform school before they get in *real* trouble." She set the box on a shelf under the counter, wiped her hands on her apron, sighed. And then to Clare's dismay she looked at her again and smiled kindly. "Sorry, honey, don't mean to ruin your meal. Not your fault what others do. Will that be all?"

Clare nodded. "Yes, ma'am" would have been more polite, she knew, but she was feeling phony enough as it was. She wished she didn't have to be the second sour note in Ginger's day; she seemed like a nice enough lady. And now she'd probably think Clare was one of *them*.

Still, the food was right in front of her, smelling so wonderful; no way she could resist it. Clare slathered the whole shebang with syrup, then made herself take her time, savoring every mouthful. She had intended to leave a little, figuring a clean dish might look too desperate, attract attention—who knew? But in the end it was all she could do to keep from licking her plate. When the last crumb was gone, she put down her fork with a sigh and made a show of picking up the green check from the counter beside her. Conscious of Ginger's eyes on her back, she slid off the stool and went to stand in line at the checkout counter.

Her timing would have to be perfect, she knew. She glanced around furtively, planning her getaway. There were two doors—an In and an Out—one on either side of the main register, where a large-nosed cashier was discussing

wart removal with a young mother who held a toddler on her hip.

"Have you tried the disks?"

"Oh, yes. They worked at first, but the darn thing came right back not two weeks later."

"Well, that happens sometimes. Personally, I prefer the liquid, though of course it's a little messier to start with. . . ."

Clare eased toward the Out door, trying her best to be invisible. Blending in, that was the first step in any disappearing act, trying not to attract attention. Stopping to look at a display of suntan lotion here, a bottle of triple-strength mouthwash there, all the time getting closer, closer to the glass-fronted exit.

"Maybe I ought to take him to the doctor and get it burned off," the customer continued, "but that sounds so painful, don't you think? Or do they just freeze them nowadays?"

"I guess it depends on the case. Bound to be expensive either way. I'd say you're better off giving this a try first."

She was almost there now. *Easy does it,* she told herself. *Slippery as oysters, smooth as smoke—no way to grab hold. Okay, that's right. You about got it licked now. Just a few steps more and you're home free—*

"Excuse me, miss." The man with the large nose was looking right at her. "Sorry to keep you waiting. I'll take care of that check for you now."

Shoot. And she had been so close! "Uh, yes, sir. I was just—just thinking about getting one of—one of these here." Clare put her hand out and picked up the first thing it touched, which turned out to be a can of Insta-Slim

37

Miracle Weight-Loss Formula: "The Delicious Way to a Slender New You." *Great. As if anybody's gonna believe that, coming from Miss Beanpole, U.S.A.*

But the cashier didn't say anything, just stood there looking at her, waiting for her to come over and settle her bill. Pulse pounding, mind racing, Clare put down the Insta-Slim and started walking back toward him. What now? Joey Morgan's money was out of the question, but what else was there? Would they let her wash dishes like in the funny papers? *Some crook you've turned out to be,* she told herself. *Some big-time criminal, striking out your very first time at the plate. Wouldn't Mama be proud?* Clare had to drag her feet, which had grown suddenly heavy; maybe she could use some of that weight-loss formula, after all. . . .

"Jackpot!" The shout startled her so that she dropped the green check before she reached the register; it sailed away on a gust of wind from the just-opened door. Clare whirled around and saw Racer and Shoe bursting back inside, waving their arms wildly. "Jackpot! Jackpot!" Racer was yelling. "Some crazy guy just hit the jackpot at Caesar's, and he's throwing money all over the boardwalk!"

"What?"

"You're kidding!"

"Not the million-dollar game!"

He might as well have shouted "Fire!" for all the confusion that followed. Customers and employees alike came flocking down the aisles, craning their heads to look out windows, crowding through the Out door.

"Come with us, Fishy," Racer whispered in Clare's ear, and the next thing she knew, he and Shoe had grabbed her arms and were pulling her out the In, just as Ginger, eyes blazing, came running from behind the counter, yelling, "Stop those kids!"

But they were too fast for her. Before Clare had time to think, she was tearing along beside the boys with the green shoes in her hands, dashing down the boardwalk as if there really were a fire behind her. Zigzagging around tourists in roller chairs and fat-bellied pigeons and guarded rest rooms, streaking past a crazy blur of Popsicle colors and dancing lights and elephants—*elephants?*—with the name Taj Mahal glittering above it all. Ducking down an alley next, checking to see that no one was following, then back-tracking—*backtracking, for crying out loud*—sometimes on the boardwalk, sometimes on side streets. Running still, still running, until her feet bled and she thought her lungs would burst for sure and her heart pound its way right out of her chest. . . .

"Whoa, Fish," said Racer, ten minutes after she knew she could go no further. "We're here."

Here was an open space with nothing but the beach on their left and a long stretch of graffiti-scrawled boards on their right: *Vegas was better/Elvis ain't coming/The King is still dead.*

Racer took another look over his shoulder to see that it was safe, nodded at Clare. "This way," he whispered. Then he pushed on a board that gave way like a gate and pulled her through to the gaping black hole on the other side.

6

THE PLACE was huge and crumbling, the half-finished shell of a parking garage that somebody must have gone broke trying to build years ago. It was damp in there, dim after the bright sunshine that had long since burned through the early-morning drizzle outside. Clare stood blinking behind the blue shades, trying to get her eyes adjusted. The floor was cold and a little slimy; no telling what was on it. She leaned over and smashed her raw feet back into the green shoes, was just straightening up when suddenly a hand was clapped over her mouth, and her arms were grabbed and pinned behind her.

"Yo, Cowboy!" somebody yelled in her ear. "They're back!"

"Sorry, Fish," Racer apologized. "Nothing personal. It's his turn for lookout, that's all. Take it easy, L.D. She's okay."

Clare was struggling in Little Dog's grasp, but she was

still out of breath and he was surprisingly strong. His hand smelled like cinnamon. Been eating Red Hots, she figured. No wonder he was so fat. Red Hots had never been a particular favorite of hers, but this was no time to be picky—

"Ow!" Little Dog let go in a hurry. "She bit me!"

Please God, she prayed, *don't let me catch something and die.*

"It's all right, L.D." Cowboy's voice came out of nowhere, everywhere, bouncing off the clammy walls, echoing through the vast, dusky spaces. Not that he was shouting; it was almost as if the shadows had spoken. "Bring her over."

Little Dog didn't dare cover her mouth again but kept hold of her arms and swore under his breath while he hustled her into the depths of the hideout, pushing her past broken bottles and rusting construction rods and crushed soda cans, all the way to a pair of large concrete blocks— throne-shaped, Clare noted, wondering if that was intended—where Cowboy sat cross-legged, chin in hand. Thimble sat opposite him, looking for all the world like a prickly blond guard dog. Clare could almost have sworn she heard growling.

Cowboy didn't appear to take much notice of her arrival. He was bent over something—a game, Clare saw as she drew nearer: a beat-up Monopoly board with half the playing pieces missing.

"Here she is," Little Dog began.

Cowboy didn't look up. "Just a second," he murmured, rattling a pair of dice. "I'm trying for doubles here." He rolled: four and four. "Out of jail free," he said, moving his man to Tennessee Avenue. He smiled now, looked at Clare. "So, how's it going?"

Amazing how an everyday question like that could make

the hairs on the back of her neck start to frizz. Who was this guy, anyhow? "Not bad, up till now," she muttered. Little Dog's fingers were cutting into her wrists. She twisted around to glare at him. "Do you mind?"

"Let her go," Cowboy ordered. "It's okay," he continued when Little Dog hesitated. "She won't run." He was studying Clare again. "There's nowhere else you have to be right now, is there—sorry, what did you say your name was?"

"I didn't," Clare answered.

Little Dog moved off a little way but continued to eye her narrowly. He pulled a pencil from behind his ear and the spiral notebook from his back pocket and commenced his infernal scribbling. Clare made a face at him, rubbed her hands on her jeans to get rid of the cinnamon smell.

Thimble poked her with a purple fingernail. "Cowboy asked your name, kid."

"Come on, Thimble." Cowboy put out his hand, gently lowered the pointing finger. "You know the rules. She doesn't have to say if she doesn't want to." He turned back to Clare. "It's up to you."

Clare shook her head.

Racer stuck his grinning face in the circle. "Me and Shoe call her Fish, don't we?"

"Hee, hee, hee!" said Shoe. *Don't he ever* talk? Clare wondered.

"Fish," Cowboy repeated, trying out the sound of it. "I guess that'll do for now—if it suits you," he added, looking at Clare.

She hung tough. "Why should I care?"

"Some people do." Cowboy leaned back. "Fish, then, for the time being. 'Course it's not a player's name. Couldn't be, not yet. That has to be earned."

"What do you mean, player?"

Cowboy didn't answer right away. He turned back to the Monopoly board, nodded at Thimble. She rattled the dice, rolled a five, and picked up her playing piece: a small silver—

"Thimble," said Cowboy, following Clare's eyes. "She's the thimble, get it? Come on, it's not too tough. Horseback rider for the Cowboy, car for the Racer, little dog for Little Dog, shoe for Shoe. This is Atlantic City, remember? One big Monopoly board, just waiting for the players. Baltic, St. Charles Place, Atlantic Avenue—you name it, it's here." He paused, pointed at the high-rent district. "And this is our turf, the prize of the lot. You got the boardwalk, Fish, you got the game."

He wasn't *serious*, was he? There was laughter sparking out of those brown eyes, surely. And yet the quiet that followed was almost reverent—like being in church, for pete's sake—the moment of silent prayer after the sermon. The only sounds were waves breaking and gulls complaining, the faraway hum of the crowd and a thin, sweet thread of music that might have been the crippled woman's keyboard:

"Over the Rainbow"—that was the tune.

Right, thought Clare. *Way over.*

Everyone seemed to be waiting for her to say something. "Well," she groped, "that's real—different. For a board game, I mean. 'Course it must be harder when you don't have all the parts—you know, fake money and property cards and all."

"What would we want with *fake* money?" It was clear that Thimble thought this was about the dumbest thing she had ever heard.

"We play our own way," Cowboy explained.

"Oh," said Clare. "Right." She took a tentative step backward. No one stopped her, so she took another, and then another. "Well, look, thanks for the help back at the drugstore. Y'all go on now, don't let me hold you up. I can find my own way out. I know how these games can go on. Seems like I heard somewhere the record was seven months or some such. . . ."

"Wait up, Fish," said Cowboy.

Clare waited. She could have made a run for it but decided against any sudden movements. *No sense spooking these nuts,* she told herself. *Best act like you would around mad dogs or crazy horses. Just don't let on you're scared, that's all.*

Cowboy looked as if he were about to say something, then appeared to change his mind. He reached in a brown bag beside him, held out a carton. "Care for an egg roll?"

The sweat from her dash down the boardwalk had finally started to dry, but now under the power of those brown eyes Clare found she was soaked again. "No, thanks," she said, but her voice sounded wimpy, and so she cleared her throat and added more loudly than she had to, "I just ate."

"Fine," said Cowboy. He took a bite himself, chewed thoughtfully for a moment. "No trouble on that score, then?"

"What score?"

"You're making out all right, I mean. Don't need any-thing—food, money maybe?" He leaned forward, lowering his voice even more. "I'm talking about real money, Fish."

Money. For a split second Clare hesitated. Lord, did she need money . . . but then the haze cleared from her brain. What did she think—that this bunch of weirdos was going to stake her to a two-hundred-dollar bus ticket? Must take at least that to get from one coast to the other. She lifted her chin. "I can take care of myself."

"Fine, then. Glad to hear it," Cowboy began, but Racer interrupted.

"She's got money, Cowboy. Five dollars. We saw it, didn't we, Shoe?"

Shoe didn't answer—no big surprise there—but before Clare could see what was coming, he had reached in her pocket with a movement so deft that she might have been brushed by butterfly wings, for all she felt it. Next thing she knew he was holding Joey Morgan's envelope in one hand and the five-dollar bill in the other, waving them high over his head and giggling that eerie giggle—"Hee, hee, hee!" Until—

Clare wheeled around and gave him a sharp elbow in the solar plexus that sent him reeling. She doubled her fists then and would have started pounding if the whole place hadn't gone crazy: Little Dog threw down his pencil and notebook and grabbed her arms again, with Racer's help this time—"Hey, man, what's wrong with you? The Shoe never hurt nobody!"—while Thimble rushed to help the kid, who was flat on his back, gasping for breath, and then she turned furiously on Clare—"Why don't you pick on somebody your own size, stilt-legs?" She would have come after Clare with her pointed purple nails if Cowboy hadn't stepped down quietly from his concrete throne just then and put a stop to the whole mess.

"All right, men, that's enough. Cool it, everybody. Nobody wants your money, Fish. You've got it all wrong."

"Tell *him* that." Clare jerked her head toward Shoe, who was still clutching his loot, even as he lay wheezing.

Cowboy walked over to him, squatted down beside him. Thimble and Racer were raising him to a sitting position, pounding him on the back.

"You all right, Shoe?" Cowboy's voice was gentle.

Shoe nodded, grinned weakly at Cowboy, then looked accusingly at Clare.

"Good man," Cowboy said. He held out his hand, and Shoe put Clare's property in it. Cowboy patted his shoulder, stood up.

"Like I said, nobody wants your money," he said, handing it to Clare. She smoothed the bill, put it back in its envelope, making a mental note to transfer it to her underwear later. "My men were only trying to make a point," Cowboy continued. "I asked them to keep an eye on you this morning, see how you made out. If they thought you looked sharp enough, their orders were to bring you back."

"And if I didn't look sharp enough?"

Cowboy shrugged. "You're here, aren't you?"

The implied compliment sent a fresh supply of blood rushing to Clare's face. *What's wrong with you?* she asked herself. *Don't make no difference what these creeps think of you.* "So what's the deal?" she growled.

"I guess it doesn't matter now, does it?" Cowboy took Clare's elbow, started guiding her toward the exit. "Looks like we made a mistake."

"What do you mean, mistake?"

"Thinking you might want to join us, you know—that you might be interested in a job. But seeing as how you're doing so well on your own, there's really no point, is there?"

They were almost to the secret opening now. Dust motes danced crazily in the slender shafts of sunlight that fell unevenly through the cracks of the piecemeal barricade. *Go on,* one part of Clare was saying, *run while you still have the chance. Who does he think he is, anyway, talking like such a big shot—some crazy kid who sleeps in playgrounds, for crying out loud, on the run, same as you. He's bluffing, that's all. He wants something from you.*

But *what?* He could see she didn't have anything, really, except Joey's five bucks, and he could have taken that if he wanted to; no matter how hard she might have fought, there were five of them and only one of her. He could have turned her out of the whale last night—*but he didn't, did he?* He gave her a place to sleep, fed her when she was hungry, which was more than she could say for some people. And if there was even a chance that he was telling the truth, if there really was money to be made somehow—why, maybe there was still a way to get to California, to find Joey Morgan, after all—

Don't be a jerk, the voice told her. *Don't trust him. Don't trust anybody.*

They had reached the opening. Cowboy peered through the broken slat, then pulled it down, held it steady. "Sorry to have wasted your time," he said.

She was halfway out before she turned around. "What kind of job?" she asked.

7

"THAT DEPENDS," said Cowboy. He waited for Clare to climb back inside. The slat closed again with a bang. "Every day's a new game. Can you follow orders?"

"Depends on the orders."

"Aw, man." Thimble looked disgusted. "I told you this was a bad idea."

"And now she's seen the *board*," Little Dog chimed in.

But Cowboy gave them a look and they closed their mouths. "No," he said, "that's fair enough." He started pacing, thinking out loud. "Say we have a test run first—see how we get along. Nothing too tough to start with . . ." He paused, let his eyes travel critically from Clare's orange spikes on down, past the blue shades and the Pink Floyd T-shirt, past the cutoff blue jeans, the dirty Bugs Bunny Band-Aid on her left shin, where she had cut herself trying to shave, all the way down to the green heels. "Nice shoes," he said.

"Thanks." Clare held her head high, but she was dying inside, horribly conscious of the dirt and blood stains around the pointed toes, the ragged places on the backs where the green material had started to pull away from the plastic underneath.

Thimble snorted. Cowboy gave her another look, and she dropped her eyes, but not before she and Clare had exchanged a look of pure poison.

"Of course you might want something a little less—dressy—for our kind of work," Cowboy went on. "Speed, that's the ticket, Fish. Shoes you can fly in, if I give the word—that's what you need."

"I can fly already."

"Sure you can. But I was thinking of something a little more—practical. Something with style, that goes without saying, but maybe more like—well, like those." He pointed to Thimble's feet, which were done up in tough-looking maroon-and-white numbers with panthers on the sides and soles built for running—the kind that fastened with Velcro tabs instead of laces. Not exactly Clare's idea of high fashion but very snug and speedy looking and man, oh, man, how her blisters would thank her. . . .

She used to have shoes like that—not as fancy maybe, but, oh, so comfortable. She had left them behind with everything else, following Joey's example: running away without a suitcase, figuring she could get whatever she really needed when they were together. How would it have looked if she had walked out carrying all her stuff? Anybody might have seen her—even Mama, getting up early to take aspirin or something, or old Peanut Breath, glancing out the window by chance on his way to the bathroom—and then where would she have been? No, she hadn't had a choice, and they were just shoes, after all, but, yes, she did miss them; she didn't miss her mother, not one bit no matter what anyone might think, but, oh, how she missed those shoes. . . .

Half an hour later she was cruising the mall with Thimble, keeping a safe distance from Cowboy and the others, who stopped off in the arcade to kill time. "Better to divide up," Cowboy had explained. "They pay less attention that way. Just do what Thimble tells you. She knows her way around."

"Hear that, kid? Whatever I say," Thimble had gloated, smiling a terrible smile.

Cowboy had seen it and said, "Don't worry, Fish. Thimble answers to me."

But that didn't mean the blond witch had to be happy about her assignment; that didn't mean she had to be nice about it. "Just follow me and don't say anything stupid," she hissed at Clare as the two of them turned into O'Farrell's department store.

"Why here?" Clare whispered. "Why not one of those shoe stores we passed already?"

"Too small. What do you want—everybody in the place staring at you?"

"I guess not."

"May I help you, ladies?"

The salesclerk in the shoe department was young and pretty, one of those perky types that was either new on the job or had watched too much morning television. Or maybe she was just early for the pageant—Miss Montana or whatever, practicing her smile for September.

"Perfect," Thimble said under her breath, just loud enough for Clare to hear. And then "Yes, please" to the

50

clerk, in a tone so close to civilized that Clare about dropped her teeth. *Please* wasn't a word she had figured to be a part of Thimble's vocabulary. "My, uh, cousin here needs a new pair of running shoes."

"Any particular brand? We have so many nice things." *Miss Montana, no question,* Clare decided. *Probably plays the accordion.*

"Whatever you recommend," said Thimble. Oh, she was smooth! "It's her birthday, you see, isn't it, cuz? And Mom said she could have anything she wants. Mom'll be here in a couple of minutes. She's over in the customer-service department, getting a couple of presents wrapped."

"Well, happy birthday!"

Good Lord. Never had Clare been so grateful for her dark glasses. "Thanks," she croaked.

"Do you know your size?"

Before Clare could answer, Thimble turned to her, smiling angelically. "What are you, cuz, about a ten and a half?"

Clare looked daggers at her. "Nine," she said. As if that weren't bad enough.

"Maybe we should measure, just to be safe," Miss Montana began, and then she saw Clare's bare feet stuck in the green heels and added, "but of course it would be better if you were wearing socks."

Clare was struck dumb at that, but Thimble was cool as cream. "Oh, Mom said we might as well pick up a few pairs while we're here—those nice cotton ones."

"Good idea," said Miss Montana, bustling off happily. When she came back, she was carrying a pair of thick socks, so glowingly white that Clare couldn't help feeling it was a shame to put her dirty feet inside them. But she did anyway, and afterwards came three pairs of sneakers, each more wonderful than the last. Clare would have been happy with any of them, but Thimble was never quite satisfied: the toe was too pointy on the first, the arch support a little lacking in the second. . . .

"Now these," said Miss Montana, stepping back to admire the third pair, "are perfect. Don't you think?"

"Perfect," Clare breathed. *Oh, man,* were they ever. There were cushions inside them, she could have sworn— goose-down pillows, little clouds of softness cuddling up to her calluses. She could run like the wind in shoes like these, fly like that florist dude with the wings on his heels—

"Nice," said Thimble, leaning down to punch Clare's big toe through the genuine aerated cowhide. "How much?"

"You're in luck," said Miss Montana, smiling so broadly that Clare was afraid she might crack something. *Did she remember to put Vaseline on her teeth?* she wondered. "Only forty-nine, ninety-nine."

Clare nearly choked. Fifty dollars for a pair of shoes? What kind of a place *was* this? It was a good thing Mama was nowhere around; she'd have laughed herself silly. Clare was too astonished to speak, but Thimble merely nodded and said, "Not bad, not bad at all. I think these are the ones. But are you sure they're big enough?" Clare started to protest, but Thimble gave her a warning look and cut her off: "You know how Mom always says you should have plenty of growing room." She smiled apologetically at Miss Montana. "Would you mind bringing us a nine and a half in this same style? Just to make sure."

"I'd be glad to," said Miss Montana, hopping right up and heading for the stockroom. She really was awfully sweet; Clare felt just terrible about having to rob her. Maybe she

should get her name and address somehow, send her a check from California once she got there. . . .

"Now," Thimble whispered, as soon as the coast was clear.

"Now what?" Clare asked.

"Now *run*, stupid!" Thimble was already on her feet, beating it past the lingerie and the perfume counter and the hand-tooled Moroccan handbags, vanishing like Houdini himself before Clare could even catch her breath.

And then it dawned on her all at once, sitting there like a piece of cheese in O'Farrell's women's shoe department; for just one moment the world stopped spinning and there were no more questions, only facts, crystal clear: she had embarked on a life of crime, and now there was no choice but to see it through. Mama was right; she was no good; she was turning out just like her real daddy, after all. There was no sense telling herself she would pay back all the people she would steal from before it was over; first it was ticket money from her mother's purse, and then it was French toast, and now it was fifty-dollar shoes, and next for all she knew it might be armored cars. And God saw every bit of it; He was up there in heaven with His giant videotape recorder or whatever it was He used and on Judgment Day He would play back this moment for the whole of creation to see: Clare Frances Caldwell (known to her underworld cronies as "Fish") sells her soul for a pair of sneakers in a ship-shaped mall in Atlantic City, New Jersey, which was without a doubt the weirdest place she had ever been in and that was even including Graceland. Talk about the dark side of the moon.

And the thing was, deep down she knew she had a choice. It wasn't as if anybody were holding a gun to her head. She could wait for Miss Montana, tell her she had changed her mind: the shoes were wonderful, but fifty bucks was way too high and it wasn't really her birthday anyway. She could put her own shoes back on and march right out the door and find Cowboy and Thimble and the rest of that peculiar gang and tell them thanks but no thanks, what they did was their business, but she had almost been confirmed once and had hell to consider. And then she could—

Could what?

Walk to California on the green spikes?

Lie on a cot next to the crippled lady and learn to play a keyboard with her tongue?

Call up Mama and Slime of the Earth and ask them to take her back?

As if she could, as if she would—

"I'm sorry," said Miss Montana, bringing out another stack of shoe boxes. "We seem to be all out of nine and a half, so I thought you might like to try—"

But Clare never heard the rest.

8

SHE LEARNED FAST after that. Not from Cowboy, so much; he had enough to worry about.

"Who crowned him king?" Clare wondered aloud once. She was only half joking, but nobody else found this at all funny.

"If it weren't for Cowboy, you'd be eating out of garbage cans by now," Thimble informed her.

Clare knew better than to listen to Thimble, but it was Little Dog who got her attention, speaking so quietly she could only just hear him: "If it weren't for Cowboy, some of us would be dead."

He wouldn't explain when Clare asked him what he meant.

Probably he was exaggerating. Absolutely. Still, the words stayed with her. And one thing was certain: Cowboy was boss. It was Cowboy all the others looked to, counting on him to make their plans, settle their disputes, answer all their most urgent questions: what they ate and when they ran and where they slept each night. Staying on the go, that was the first rule, making sure their tracks were covered.

"Never sink into a pattern. That leaves you wide open. Keep 'em guessing. Ever wonder why the cops around here don't know if there's three of us or three hundred? Because we never make the same move twice, that's why."

He was talking about hideouts, mainly. The playground was still good every now and again, but if they had used it too many nights running, someone would have been sure to notice. Same with the half-finished garage, which was Thimble's favorite spot for some reason, probably just because it gave Clare the creeps, with its dank empty spaces and unexplained scurryings—the *real* mammoth rats, Thimble assured her. Clare tried to turn a deaf ear to these scare tactics, but the truth was she much preferred any of the half dozen other places the gang had laid claim to— condemned and abandoned houses, mostly, in the decaying neighborhood that stretched for block after crumbling block just out of sight of the swankiest casinos, so close you could practically hear the slot machines ringing.

There was one in particular—an old wreck of a place on Baltic Avenue—that felt almost homey, once you made your way past the broken glass and rotting garbage and maybe a passed-out drunk or two on the sidewalk outside, then climbed in through the boarded-up window that Little Dog had pried loose with a tire iron. Whoever had lived there last had left in such a hurry that they hadn't bothered to pack much of their stuff—junk, mostly, but there were some nice touches: a paint-by-numbers rendering of a wall-eyed horse, a few old chairs with the stuffing spilling from their faded upholstery, a yellow lamp with ceramic bananas

56

growing out of its sides. This lamp had no light bulb, and of course even if there had been one, there was no electricity, but Clare was fond of it anyway. Sitting beside it, she could almost imagine she had just *decided* not to turn it on, that if she felt like it, she could flip the rusted switch and the whole place would be flooded with warm yellow light, the loveliest light you ever saw.

The dark still bothered her, bothered her more than ever these nights. It was then that ghosts with pink-rimmed pig's eyes came looking for her, groping with greasy fingers. She couldn't have stood it if it weren't for the flashlights Cowboy had stashed in each hideout. They had to be used sparingly, he said; no better way to make the cops come running than to set beams of light dancing around a supposedly empty place. But at least they were *there*; at least she knew that if she had one of those bad spells when the darkness started breathing on her, choking her with the stench of peanuts, why, then she could do something about it. But mostly it was just the *idea* of light that she found comforting.

"Where do you go when it gets cold?" she asked once. It wasn't cold that night—not in the middle of June—just a little breezy, with the salt wind blowing in off the ocean. But that wind had set her wondering.

Racer and Little Dog exchanged nervous glances at that, and no one answered until Thimble spoke up testily: "Don't worry about it. Cowboy has it all figured. You just do your job. He'll take care of the rest."

No, Cowboy had a lot on his mind, so it was Thimble who was assigned to teach her, more often than not—not graciously but thoroughly: how to stake out the lower-quality restaurants and pick up tips before the waitresses saw them, how to hawk lucky numbers to superstitious gamblers outside the casinos, how to lift whole handfuls of fake jewelry from the bins at Captain Billy's Trash 'n Treasure, then sell them to idiot tourist kids on the beach and run before their parents pounced—

Oh, yes, *run*—zipping along in her new winged sneakers, which were all she had hoped for and more: lighter than air, more full of bounce than a trampoline. She had been fast before, but now she was a comet, a meteor.

Cowboy hadn't been lying about the money. It was here, all right, all over this island—money for the taking, riding in with tourists by the busload, itching to be spent, burning great holes in its owners' pockets. Not that the would-be gamblers were rich, for the most part; mostly they were decidedly *un*rich looking: old people with varicose veins and receding hairlines, wrinkled women and bald-headed men with knit shirts stretched tightly over their potbellies. Not smiling much, any of them, just plodding politely from casino to casino, with numbers trailing out of their mouths like kite tails:

"They say the Claridge pays double odds on craps. . . . Played the quarter machines at Bally's once and went eleven straight hours on fourteen seventy-five. . . . I hear he spent over a billion dollars on that Taj Mahal. . . . As far as I'm concerned, it isn't worth a nickel. . . ."

"Are they having any *fun*?" Clare asked Racer.

"Naw, man," he explained. "They just *think* they are."

She started to feel really crummy then, when the gang pulled one of its scams. The ketchup caper was the worst. Oh, it *sounded* simple enough:

"You and me go walking down the boardwalk, see," Thimble coached her, "talking up a storm, get it? And we'll both be carrying french fries—a couple bags apiece. We act like we're not looking where we're going, but all the time we got our eye on some blue-haired lady and her old man, see what I'm saying? Then first chance we get, we smack right into 'em, like it's an accident, which of course it ain't, and we spill ketchup all over the old lady. That's when we really turn it on—apologizing like crazy, pulling out wads of paper napkins, trying to clean her up, see, while her old man gets all red in the face and stands there yelling at everybody. Only here's the deal: while he's shooting off his mouth, old Shoe's gonna be in and out of his pocket so fast this guy ain't even gonna know he's been hit, won't have a clue till it's too late. By then we're long gone—down at the Central Pier maybe, riding the Super-Loops. See what I'm saying?"

Clare saw, all right. No piddling little venial sin this time; this was flat-out mortal, no question about it. She could already read the card Saint Peter would hand her:

> GO TO HELL
> GO DIRECTLY TO HELL
> DO NOT PASS PEARLY GATES
> DO NOT COLLECT ETERNAL REWARD

But no amount of seeing could have prepared her for the real-life victims: a wispy grandmother and her apple-cheeked husband, who looked a little like old Father Cavanaugh back home, for crying out loud, with his mild gray eyes and liver spots. And as if that weren't bad enough, they didn't even get mad about the ketchup:

"Quite all right, no harm done."

"Thank you, young lady, but don't bother. We'll just run into Caesar's here for some water. I'm sure it'll wash right out."

"No, no, never mind, quite all right. . . ."

It was Racer who found her afterward, sitting on the grungy shag rug beneath the banana lamp, sobbing into her new black stretch pants. She had bought them less than an hour before with her share of the stolen money; she had thought she really needed them, but already they were hateful to her. She would never be able to wear them without thinking of that sweet old couple.

"Why did they have to be so—so durn *nice* about it?" she blubbed, unable to stop her tears.

"Come on, Fish, forget it," Racer said, sitting down beside her. He tried to pat her shoulder, but she pulled away; she didn't deserve to be comforted, and anyhow she didn't like guys touching her.

But Racer wouldn't let it go. "You just have to put it out of your head, that's all. Like old Shoe, see there? Think he's worried?"

Shoe was sitting in one of the ratty chairs, humming softly to himself, playing with a Slinky toy he had picked up at Kay-Bee after the score. Flipping it happily from hand to hand, back and forth, back and forth. Maybe he wasn't all there upstairs, but Clare couldn't help envying him his happy lack of anything resembling a conscience.

"Naw," Racer went on, "Shoe knows the game. It's just business, see, like old Al Pacino said in that movie, remember? It ain't personal."

"Al *Pacino*? The freakin' *godfather*? Good Lord, Racer!"

"Aw, cut the whining." Thimble looked up from her nail filing. "Ain't you ever heard of Darwin?"

"Darwin who?"

"Darwin—you know—survival of the fittest. It's us or them, that's all. We can play by their rules and end up in the County Dump for Troubled Teens or whatever. Or we can make up our own rules as we go. At least then we have a fighting chance."

"But those old people—they hardly had anything. Thirty bucks in that wallet, that's all, and those dumb pictures of their grandkids. . . ." Clare's nose was running. She wiped it roughly on her sleeve. She used to have a grandmother, a long time ago.

"They had a MasterCard in that wallet, too, don't forget." Little Dog was lying on his back in the corner—napping, Clare had assumed till then—with his notebook spread open over his face. "At least they have credit."

"Yeah, sure"—Clare was still gulping for air—"but not all that much. It wasn't even the g-gold kind."

"You're not thinking straight, Fish." Now Cowboy was there, though Clare could have sworn he hadn't been just a minute before. He came and went like smoke sometimes; you wouldn't even know he was around, and then suddenly the shadows would speak: "All those old people—they come to this island *expecting* to get cleaned out. It's guaranteed. They're gonna lose that money one way or another. Better it goes to us than Donald Trump."

"But they ain't *all* losers—not every one. Some of 'em might win."

"Don't kid yourself, kid." Little Dog slid the notebook off his face, raised himself on one elbow. "Ever see an odds maker's book? In the long run, everybody loses. It's built into the numbers. That's how the casinos survive."

"Believe it, Fish." Cowboy's voice was low. He paused,

fixed Clare with his brown eyes. "Nobody wins in Atlantic City."

Silence. The heat in the old house seemed suddenly oppressive, in spite of the ocean breeze slipping in through the cracks of the boarded-up windows.

" 'Cept us, right, Cowboy?" Racer gave his shoulders a playful shove. "Nobody wins but us."

Cowboy didn't answer right away. *He looks tired*, Clare thought. And then was surprised at herself for thinking such a thing. *Why be surprised?* she wondered. *He's human, ain't he?*

But then he turned to Racer, began to laugh quietly. "Right," he said. "Nobody but us."

9

CLARE HARDLY NOTICED the red-haired man at first. She had slipped away from the others for a while, gone for a walk, hoping the salt air would clear some of the demons out of her brain. After a bit she stopped and bought herself a Coke. She was sipping it, leaning up against the back of one of the blue-and-white boardwalk benches, gazing out at the water, when the voice over her right shoulder made her turn:

"Doesn't make much sense, does it?"

"Excuse me?" She was too surprised to be frightened. Strangers didn't usually speak to her out of the blue, no matter what the fairy tales preached.

"These benches—they're backward, haven't you noticed? Here they go to the trouble of building a whole city right beside an ocean, and then they nail down all the benches facing *away* from it. Crazy, huh?"

He could have passed for a TV newscaster or a young

politician—one of those clean-cut, confident guys the cameras love. His thick red hair was neatly combed, shining in the last of the afternoon sun. His clothes (a suit and tie, yet, in Atlantic City!) were cool without being flashy; something rich about the cut or the materials maybe—Clare couldn't have said just what.

The man smiled, and Clare found herself smiling back. He reminded her of Joey Morgan, just a bit. Not in the way he looked, exactly, but in the way he looked at *her*—as if he were actually *interested* in her opinion of the benches. Which did seem pretty silly, now that she thought about it.

"I guess so," she murmured.

The man's smile grew wider. "Now there's an accent you don't hear around this town too often! Don't tell me—North Carolina, right?"

"No, sir. Te—Texas." Clare caught herself at the last second.

"Is that right? Texas, huh? The Lone Star State."

"Yes, sir."

"Well, that's great. Been to San Antonio a time or two myself. Interesting place. You know, Davy Crockett, the Alamo . . ."

"Mmm-hmm." Lord. Clare hoped he wasn't going to quiz her on Texas history. He seemed nice and all, but maybe it was time to be moving on. Still, she couldn't just turn and run, could she? That would look suspicious.

The red-haired man took out a cigarette, offered her one. She shook her head, and he grinned. "Good girl," he said. "Just testing you. I'm trying to quit myself." He lit up, blew a smoke ring over his head. "Here on vacation, huh?"

"Yes, sir."

"Terrific. With your folks, I guess?"

"Uh, that's right. They're—they're just down at Bally's. Playing the slots."

"Great. Hope they're winning, hmm? Maybe you'll get a trip to the mall out of it anyway. Bet you'd like that."

Clare didn't say anything. The red-haired man waited for a second, then went right on:

"I guess this place gets a little dull for you sometimes, doesn't it? At least, that's what my niece tells me. She says there's nothing much to do around here if you're under eighteen."

"Well . . ."

"You know, the two of you ought to get together, have some fun. Catch a movie maybe. You like movies? My niece is crazy about 'em. I'll bet you're about the same age—don't tell me—fourteen?"

"N-no . . ." This was going too far. She had to get out of here, whether it looked funny or not. She hadn't finished her Coke, but she tossed it in the nearest basket, started to back away.

The red-haired man followed. "No? Fifteen, then? Or, no—thirteen, am I right? They grow 'em tall in Texas, I forgot."

"Yeah—no—" Clare was really getting nervous now. Maybe those fairy tales had something, after all. "Look, I gotta go."

The red-haired man reached out, grasped her wrist. His hand was warm. "No, you don't. Not really. Where would you go? Tell the truth, now. Your parents aren't at Bally's, are they?"

"You don't know what you're talking about." Clare tried

65

to pull away, but there was surprising strength in his grip, something almost paralyzing in the friendly pressure of those warm fingers.

"Don't I?" His smile was gentle now. "Easy, just take it easy, sweetheart. You don't have to look so scared. I'm not a policeman, if that's what you're afraid of. You're not in any trouble. I want to help, that's all. Bet you haven't had a decent meal in weeks, have you?"

"Lay off, Griffey."

It was Cowboy. Clare and the red-haired man spun around and saw him at the same time. She didn't know where he had come from, or how he happened to be there; she only knew she had never been so glad to see anyone in her entire life.

The red-haired man seemed glad, too. "Well, look who's here!" he said, still holding on to Clare's wrist. "My old friend Warren! Didn't know you were still around, buddy. What's up?"

Warren? Is that his real name?

"I said lay off, Griffey. Let her go." Cowboy's voice was dangerously quiet. He wasn't quite as tall as the other guy, and he was a good twenty pounds lighter. But Clare would have put even money on him, if fists had started flying.

The red-haired man said nothing for a moment. He was smiling still, looking at Cowboy as if the two of them shared some marvelous joke.

Cowboy moved in closer. "I'm not kidding, man."

The red-haired man laughed out loud, let go of Clare. He held up both hands, as if he were being arrested. "No sweat, buddy. I was just worried about the young lady, that's all. Didn't realize she was a friend of yours." He took a drag on his cigarette, dropped it to the boardwalk, stubbed it out with the sole of his shiny wing-tipped shoe. "Liking 'em younger these days, hmm? I thought that blond was more your style."

"Shut up, Griffey."

"Come on, Warren, where's your sense of humor? Don't give your new girlfriend the wrong idea. We had some good times together, didn't we?"

Cowboy didn't say anything to that, just gave the red-haired man a dirty look and started walking away, grabbing Clare's *other* wrist—*Lord*, this was getting old—and pulling her along with him.

Griffey's laughter followed them. "Who'da thought it?" he called. "Sweet little Warren, a ladies' man!"

They walked along in silence for as long as Clare could stand it. She thought she would die of shame if someone didn't say something pretty soon, but Cowboy didn't look as if he were about to help her out.

"Thanks," she muttered finally.

No answer.

She waited a minute, tried again. "I was gonna run. I was just about to, but he—he said some things—about the cops. So I was, you know, looking for the right time."

Cowboy didn't even glance her way, just kept pulling her along beside him. Clare had had enough of this. She jerked her hand away.

He stopped and looked at her now—the bug-under-the-microscope routine again—then walked on without her.

Clare watched him for a few seconds. *Who does he think he is?* Then she ran to catch up. "Look, I *said* thanks."

Cowboy kept going. "Didn't anybody ever teach you not to talk to strangers?" At least he was speaking now. Or growling, maybe; that was more like it.

67

She looked at him sideways. "*You* seemed to know him."

It was the wrong thing to say. Cowboy stopped again, only this time the look on his face made her take a step back; for a split second she thought he was going to hit her. But he never raised his hand, just stood there for a minute, glaring at her. And then he began to speak again in that low, terrible voice:

"Listen, you don't know anything about me, you got that? And I don't know anything about you—not your name or how you got here or why you came. And I don't *want* to know, see? That's not any of my business. You want to forget whatever crud's behind you—well, fine. Who doesn't? But you're *here* now, get it? You ain't back in Kansas with Auntie Em or whoever. You've come to a tough town, but you're with us. You'll be all right if you use your head and *stick* with us. You can't go off half-cocked by yourself, not on this island. You can't go trusting every jerk you meet."

Cowboy paused, ran his fingers through his hair, glanced back down the boardwalk. "Guys like Griffey," he continued, spitting out the words as if they had a bad taste, "they feed off people like us. It doesn't matter how nice their clothes are or what straight teeth they have or any of that. They're scum, is what they are. They're only interested in what they can get out of you, understand what I'm saying? In what they can make you do. And they'll tell you they're your friends, but it's a lie. You're garbage to them, nothing more. And if you let them, pretty soon they'll have you believing you're garbage, too."

Clare thought of Sid and his greasy fingers. A shiver ran through her. She felt sick to her stomach, clammy skinned.

That was what the red-haired man had wanted, then. What Sid had wanted.

"Do you understand me?"

Clare nodded. There was something wrong with her throat; it seemed to have swollen to the size of a young tree trunk.

"All right, then." The jagged edge had worn off Cowboy's tone. He looked suddenly weary, as if he had aged twenty years in the last twenty minutes.

Nothing else was said on the walk back to the Baltic house. The memory of the red-haired man was a dead weight between them—an awkward sort of burden that had to be lugged along like a sack of refuse. It took all their energy, kept them from looking at each other, even. But just before they climbed in through the boarded-up window, Cowboy stopped once more, cleared his throat.

"Listen," he said, "I'd appreciate it if you wouldn't mention any of—you know, what happened back there. To the others, I mean."

Clare shrugged, tried out her voice. "Ain't nothing to mention, is there?"

Cowboy gave her a ghost of a smile. "Not a thing," he said.

10

THIMBLE WAS WAITING for them. "Where have you two been?" she asked, giving Clare her usual welcoming scowl.

Clare shrugged. "Nowhere," she said.

"Out," said Cowboy. He walked right past her, flung himself in one of the old chairs. He closed his eyes.

Thimble put her hands on her hips. *Fierce*, that was the word for her; she looked like a volcano about to erupt. Clare wouldn't have been all that surprised if her head had started smoking. "So which is it?" she demanded. "Nowhere or out?"

"Give it a rest, Thimble." Cowboy sounded too tired to argue. "It really doesn't matter."

"Maybe not to *you*." Thimble gave the chair a swift kick, and then another. "Maybe nothing matters to you no more. But it matters to me, do you hear me? It matters to me." And she kicked the chair again and again, until her sneaker tore through the worn material to the ancient stuffing inside. When she brought it out this time, the entire shoe was covered with little bits of moldy gray fluff. She tried to shake it off, but the stuff stuck. And then without warning her mouth was working strangely and her eyes were spurting tears, though she tried not to show it; she turned away, sat down on the shag rug, and started pulling lint off her shoe. "It matters to me," she repeated bitterly, in a small, choked voice.

Cowboy sighed. He rose from the chair, stood there for a minute, looking down at Thimble's back, at the blond frizz quivering ever so slightly, the shoulders hunched over her task. And then he sat down beside her, and very gently, even tenderly, he took the sneakered foot in his hands and began to remove the fuzz.

A sudden rush of—what?—some kind of heat in the back of her neck, the tips of her ears, made Clare turn away in—*what?* Confusion, embarrassment maybe—yes, certainly embarrassment; it couldn't be anything else, could it? Not *jealousy*, no way; *she* wasn't jealous. Not of *Thimble*, for crying out loud, not of Thimble and *Cowboy*. Good Lord. She was tired, that was all, flustered after her scare with that awful red-haired man; her feelings were turned inside out. Maybe she was coming down with something, feeling a little feverish, that was all. Probably she was catching a stupid cold.

Whatever it was, it stayed with her long past dark, made the Whopper she ate later turn to a leaden lump in her stomach. It didn't matter whether her eyes were open or closed; she kept seeing it again: Cowboy's hands reaching out, cradling that dirty sneaker with such amazing tender-

71

ness. And then that same odd feeling would shoot up the back of her neck, paralyzing her, singeing her, practically, with its heat.

"Don't worry about Thimble," Racer told her late that night, while the others were sleeping. They had just moved back to the playground a few hours before. Clare was sitting in the whale's mouth, looking out at the lopsided moon, when he crawled out of the sea lion and joined her. "She's crazy, that's all. Chased off I don't know how many other girls before you came along. Trouble with Thimble, she thinks everybody and her sister is out to take Cowboy away. Shoot, sometimes she kinda looks at *me* crooked. How weird is that?" Racer chuckled. "You just can't pay her no mind, that's all."

"What do you mean, crazy? What's her problem, anyhow?"

"I don't know, Fish. We ain't supposed to talk about—whatever came before. . . ." Racer looked around, then continued in a lower voice. "But seems like it ain't exactly fair, with you coming so much later, and her always treating you like dirt. Look, all I know is, she was hurtin' pretty bad when Cowboy found her. That was over a year ago now. Somebody had got to her. She was black-and-blue all over—couldn't hardly tell she was a girl, even. Mumbling something about—I don't know, some real bad dude—wasn't no telling what she was saying. Had him mixed up with her daddy some way. Or maybe he *was* her daddy, I don't know. But Cowboy, he don't make nobody explain nothing, he just takes her in, that's all, takes care of her. Just like he done with the Dog when he found him trying to make it by hisself. Kid was about to starve to death, do you believe that? Didn't have a clue. That's when Cowboy gives him the first of them notebooks he's so crazy about, tells him he needs one of them whaddya call 'em, accountants, somebody to keep our records straight. Don't ask me why, never seemed like they needed to be straight before. But the weird part is, it worked. Seemed like it was all the Dog needed someway, that one little thing. And old Thimble—well, I guess maybe Cowboy's the first person ever was nice to her. So she goes kinda, whaddya call it—overboard, you know? You heard of people being nuts about somebody? Well, that's Thimble—only I mean *really* nuts. Thinks she's, I don't know—in love or whatever, you tell me."

Clare was quiet for a moment, thinking this over. The first person ever was nice to her—like Joey Morgan, maybe; that was what Joey Morgan had been for Clare. That was different, of course; Joey was so much older, more like a real father. Still, it helped her understand a little, why Thimble cared so much, why she was so afraid of losing what she had.

And then the picture came into her head once more: Cowboy's hands on the fuzzy sneaker. And again it followed, that sick, hot feeling—

"And—Cowboy?" she murmured, drawing a circle in the sand at her feet, too ashamed of her scorched face to lift it. "Does he feel—that way—about her?"

"Cowboy?" The question seemed to surprise Racer. "You tell me, man. Nobody knows nothin' 'bout what old Cowboy's thinking. Sometimes, though—" He paused, as if he were considering whether or not he should go on.

"Sometimes what?"

"I don't know, Fish. Sometimes I wonder, is all—'bout what it was musta happened to him, what coulda made him like he is, you know? Thinking he got to watch out for the whole world, take care of every hard case he runs across. I mean, you can see for yourself, he don't act like nobody else. Other dudes his age—what do you figure, he's fifteen, sixteen maybe?—mosta them others, street kids, I'm talking about, they're heavy into all kinds of crud—weed, booze, and a lot worse than that—anything they can put their hands on. I ain't blaming 'em, not me. I used to figure, whatever makes you feel okay for a while, well, why not? But Cowboy, he don't go for that stuff. He's clean as my mama's kitchen sink. Don't even smoke, man, won't have it around him. One time old Thimble, she jimmies the lock on one of them machines, helps herself to a pack of Camels. And Cowboy, he really reads her, says what can she be thinking, putting that crud in her body? Gonna dull her senses, man, make her weak and stupid—what then? Anybody could come along, take advantage someway, who knows? Naw, old Cowboy, he says you got to stay sharp to survive in this place, got to have some discipline, that's the only way. So Thimble, she don't want nothing more than pleasing him. She throws them ciggies away and never looks back."

Clare nodded. She was thinking of the red-haired man again, of the cigarette he had offered her. She was glad she hadn't taken it. . . . She shivered a little, put the thought behind her. She looked sideways at Racer. He had picked up a piece of seashell, starting filling in the circle she had started. Turning it into a clown, it looked like, with a silly smile and a big blob of a nose and a ruffled collar beneath the chin.

She was grateful for his company. Racer was the only one who had ever talked to her much, really talked to her.

The only one who ever seemed to want to talk at all. Or was it more than just wanting—was it *needing* to talk? The thought surprised her somehow. Racer was always so happy-go-lucky, laughing at everything. Nothing ever seemed to bother him. He had Shoe, of course; they were joined at the hip, practically. Oh, sure, he could talk to Shoe all he wanted. But maybe it got kind of lonesome, now and then, talking to someone who never talked back.

"What about you, Racer?" Clare asked now. "How'd you and Shoe get hooked up with this bunch?"

Racer ignored the first part of the question. He smiled. "Shoe?" he replied. "Old Shoe, he's all right now, ain't he? Over there this minute, sleeping like a newborn baby. Used to be, he could never sleep like that. Back at the old place he was all the time waking up, screaming fit to raise the dead." Racer paused again, added a fancy tassel to his clown's hat. "Who knows, maybe that was what he was trying to do."

"Raise the *dead*? What's that supposed to mean?"

Racer sighed. "They said there'd been a fire. All his folks—mama, daddy, coupla sisters, all fast asleep—burned up, ever' last one. Even the dog—Hazel, that was the name he used to holler in his sleep. They said it was her caused the fire, chewing through some kind of electrical wire. Firemen came, but it was too late—except for Shoe, and he was burned pretty bad. That's why his skin looks so funny."

Good Lord. "But wait—you said he was calling the dog's name. You mean he can talk? I thought—"

"Naw, man, Shoe ain't a mute. Just don't see the point in talking anymore, I guess. I don't know, maybe he just got sick of it after a while—all them doctors at that place, asking all the same questions, over and over—"

"What place?"

Racer shrugged. The clown in the sand was juggling now—oranges maybe—and hopping around on bowed legs. "Just a place, don't matter. One of them outfits where they send kids with whaddya call 'em, behavior difficulties. Old Georgie—Shoe, I mean—he was behaving pretty difficult, all right. Giving 'em fits, that was what he was doing. Used to be you could tell real easy whose turn it was to take care of him. They'd be scratched all to pieces, chunks taken out of 'em sometimes." Racer chuckled. "One big tall dude had his ear bandaged for a week. Word was Georgie had tried to bite it off. Shoe, I mean. Thinka that—old Shoe, who wouldn't hurt a fly no more, even if it bit *him* first. He just wanted out, you see. That was all he was trying to say."

Were they *all* damaged, then? Every single one? Even— "You were in that place, too? The place for kids with— problems?"

It was as if an invisible door had swung shut between them. Racer stared at her blankly for a minute, then looked away, started wiping out his bowlegged clown. "Shoot, man, sometimes they make mistakes, that's all. Weren't nothing wrong with me, don't know what they were thinking." He heaved his arm back, tossed his shell far out into the darkness. When he looked at Clare again, he was grinning. "'Course I didn't hang around there for long. Hit the road first chance I got—just like in the movies. *Escape From Alcatraz*—you ever see that one? Only I didn't have to worry about sharks and all. Took old Shoe with me. He's been laughing ever since. Freakin' doctors, I coulda told 'em all along."

Clare didn't know what to say, so she didn't say anything. The two of them sat for a while more, watching the moon climb higher in the eastern sky. A mist had sprung up from the sea, shrouding it in a soft white glow.

"Ring around the moon means the fairies will be dancing," she said—more to herself than to Racer, really. But he laughed out loud.

"Who told you that?"

Clare blushed. "Somebody. Nobody. It was a long time ago."

"Shoot, man." Racer blew a sand tick off his arm. "Ain't no fairies in New Jersey."

11

IT WAS a perfect summer's day. Miss Montana was walking down the boardwalk, carrying a string of fish over her shoulder. Clare panicked and tried to hide, but Miss Montana had already spotted her. She smiled and waved her over.

"Look what I caught," she said, and as she held out her prize for Clare to see, she winked slyly, and the fish changed into birds—beautiful birds that flew away, filling the sky with their rainbow-colored wings, while Clare and the lady laughed and laughed. . . .

"Hey, Fish! Wake up, man! It's a party!"

"Go away." Clare rolled over on her side, covered her face with her arm. Now she'd never find her way back into that dream, and it had been such a fine one, the best all month—no greasy-fingered, red-haired monsters chasing her, for a change.

"Come on, Fish, I know you hear me. I said it's a party!"

"Leave me alone, Racer. Good Lord. It's the middle of the night."

"Naw, man, it ain't all that late, not even eleven yet. You act like my old lady, don't want to do nothing but sleep."

It was partly true; seemed as if she was always tired these days. Maybe because when she did sleep, it was with her eyes and ears half-open, never really resting. She had to be ready to run if danger threatened, if the wind shifted suddenly and Cowboy smelled cops, like he had done just last night in the playground. They were back in the old garage again now, cuddled up with the crushed Coke cans and invisible rats.

Couldn't be that there was trouble tonight, though, with Racer grinning like he didn't have good sense and Shoe right beside him with his giggle motor running: "Hee, hee, hee!"

"Please, y'all, just let me sleep. I don't want to go to a party."

"Naw, Fishy, you don't get it. At this party, you can sleep all you want."

"What are you talking about?"

Racer beamed. "Cowboy scored us a motel room, that's what I'm talking about. Two queen-size beds and our own toilet, right, Shoe? And a ice machine and a television and I don't know what all else—room service maybe, if we feel like it. Paid in full till noon tomorrow."

Clare was sitting up now. "You're kidding me."

"Aw, man, come on, check it out, then you tell me if I'm kidding."

Someway or other, Cowboy had done it. Clare could

only guess how. Used the fake ID he carried for emergencies, she supposed, paid with cash from the latest job, whatever he could get out of Little Dog. L.D. was tighter than the lid on a pickle jar, and even then the cash had a way of trotting out twice as fast as it trickled in. But there was no way he would ever have refused Cowboy anything.

Besides, it wasn't as if he had demanded the High Roller's Suite at the Taj Mahal. This place was of the pretty-much-gone-to-seed variety, one of those chintzy numbers that had been built along the boardwalk years and years ago most likely; it still displayed an old neon AIR-COOLED BY REFRIGERATION sign. There was a just-beginning-to-peel coat of flamingo pink paint on everything, inside and out, and a suspicious musty smell coming from the wheezing window unit. But it was a regular paradise after the whale and the banana lamp.

The first sound Clare heard when she came in the door (they sneaked through one at a time, since Cowboy was only paying for two—him and his "wife") was the toilet flushing.

"Shoe," Racer explained. "He takes off the tank top and watches how it works. You'll see, he'll go twenty times before it gets light."

Thimble actually smiled at that. Lord in heaven, she wasn't in a *good mood*, was she? It seemed too much to hope for, but there she was, wearing an almost pleasant expression, sprawled out beside Cowboy on one of the big beds. They were watching an old "Beverly Hillbillies" rerun on the television—good old dumb wonderful laugh-tracking boob-tubing TV, no more reassuring sound in the universe. Clare felt herself blushing with pleasure; it was almost embarrassing how much she had missed it. And there was Little Dog, too, sitting on the other bed, doling out slices of pizza from a cardboard box: pepperoni and mushrooms and onions and green peppers and *olives*, even; Clare loved olives, but nobody else ever wanted them. Oh, pizza and television and clean sheets and a tub waiting and *olives*, too—talk about the lap of luxury. Racer was right; this really *was* a party!

There wasn't much talking at first, just the comforting drone of the TV and chewing sounds and the occasional clatter of ice falling in the machine outside. But then Racer gave Clare a look, put a finger to his lips, and slipped a quarter in the slot on Cowboy's headboard that turned on the "Magic Fingers" in his mattress. "What the—" Cowboy and Thimble shouted at once, which somehow struck the others as hilarious, and before long everybody was trying it out and laughing their heads off because it was such a gyp, nothing to it really, just a lot of dumb jiggling. But they all loved it, Shoe especially; he was laughing like crazy—

Until all of a sudden his eyes got really big and he jumped off the bed and ran into the bathroom, and in a minute the others could hear the sound of the toilet flushing again.

"You think he's all right?" Thimble asked.

Little Dog looked worried, too. "Too much pizza, maybe," he suggested.

But Racer said, "Naw, man, ain't no such thing as too much pizza. Old Shoe's just checking out his favorite hobby, that's all." And sure enough, a few minutes later Shoe was back, smiling.

They fooled around with the remote control for the television then, switching it endlessly from one channel to the next, watching silly snatches of this and that: a parakeet eating birdseed off its owner's tongue, a woman in a string bikini telling a man in a suit that her ideal mate was Albert Einstein except for the hair, a skinny young Frank Sinatra cracking wise in an old war movie—

"Naw, leave it here!" Racer shouted when Cowboy started to switch once more. "It's Frank, man! *From Here to Eternity!*"

Thimble groaned. "Not Frank Sinatra again—quick, change it before he tells the story."

"What story?" Clare asked.

Groans all around now, except from Racer and Shoe, whose faces were shining. "Ain't I ever told you about the time I met Frank?" asked Racer.

"Say yes," Little Dog whispered loudly, but she shook her head.

"Aw, man, it was the best. There we were, just me and Shoe, working the boardwalk. This was before we met up with the others, see, lot more dangerous back then. And here come this old lady in a yellow wig, just bopping along looking rich as cake, right next to this guy all duded up in one of them big old whaddya call 'em, trench coats. You know, collar all pushed up around his neck, shades like yours, Fish, real mysterious-like. 'Course I don't pay him no mind at first. I'm too busy making my move on the old lady.

"Oh, we're pretty slick, all right, ain't we, Shoe? Sliding in like them dudes in the Ice Capades. First thing you know the wig lady's got ketchup all over. 'Eek!' she's saying. 'Oh, my, oh, my!' 'What's wrong, honey?' says the man in the coat. 'What's going on here?' 'Coupla young punks,' says the lady. 'Look what they done to my cashmere sweater!' 'Sorry, lady,' I say. 'Wish I could kick myself, but I got this bum knee here, makes me sorta clumsy. Here now, lemme sponge you off. You want I should pay for the cleaner's?'

"But the man, he says, 'Forget it, kid, go on now. We'll take care of it.'

" 'You sure, mister? I'm awful sorry. Looka here now, here's a spot I missed.'

" 'I said forget it, kid. You got ears or what?'

"So Shoe and me, we beat it like he says, don't stop running till we hit Mediterranean. Then Shoe hands me the guy's wallet and I look inside and like to faint and fall out, 'cause what's it say on the first card staring back at me?"

"Richard Simmons?" Clare teased.

"Madonna," Thimble suggested, hitting Racer over the head with a pillow.

"Elmer Fudd?" Another pillow from Little Dog.

"Naw, listen!" Racer protested. "It was Frank, man! Spelled out right there in them bumpy little letters on his American Express. Francis A. Sinatra, blam, blam, blam, don't leave home without it." Racer climbed to the top of the pillow pile, raised both arms over his head in a V for victory.

"Hee, hee, hee!" laughed Shoe.

"So what'd you do with it?" Clare asked.

The others all groaned again and fell back on the mattresses, holding their ears.

Racer grinned. "I gave it back," he said.

"Hee, hee, hee!"

"You *gave it back*?"

"That's what I said, little Fishy." Racer was standing on the bed now, strutting like a peacock. "I gave it back." He made a flourish with his hand, took a bow.

"Ow!" said Thimble. "Watch it, buster, you're stepping on me."

"Sorry, lady, but I got this bum knee—"

The pillow attack started again.

"Wait," said Clare, "was there money inside?"

"Money? You kidding me? Musta been two—three hundred dollars in cash. We're talking Sinatra, man!"

Little Dog shook his head. "Kind of puts a whole new twist on that Robin Hood deal. Rob from the rich, give it right back."

Racer smiled a lofty smile. "L.D.'s just jealous, that's all. This wasn't just any old rich guy. This was *Frank*, man, Ol' Blue Eyes hisself. You can't steal from him, no way. That'd be, I don't know, unpatriotic or something."

"But how'd you do it?" Clare asked. "How'd you ever find him again?"

"No problem, was it, Shoe? We just went over to the Sands. That was where he was doing his show. The guard, he tried to stop us at the front door, but I say, 'Better let us in, man. We got business with Mr. S.' And then I show him the wallet, and next thing you know, me and Shoe's sitting there in Frank's suite—now there was a *room*, man—having a glass of ginger ale and chewing on a couple whad-dya call 'em, club sandwiches. You know, the ones they cut up fancy and then stick back together with them cute little swords. Ain't we, Shoe?"

"Hee, hee, hee!"

"And Frank—he's looking just like he *looks*, you know? Without the shades and all, I mean. Saying, 'Well, well, my young friends, how can I ever thank you? Lucky for me it was you who found my wallet. Ain't too many people woulda done what you done.' But me, I'm cool, I say, 'Naw,

Frank, forget it, man. It was our pleasure. The drinks, the food, this time we had together—you done enough already.' So Frank, he says, 'Well, thanks again, gentlemen. You keep in touch now, you hear? And if there's ever anything I can do for you, you just let me know.' So then we shake hands, and that's that."

Thimble stuck her head out from under the pillow she had buried it in. "Is he done yet?"

"All done," said Racer, taking another bow.

"No way," said Clare.

"Don't believe a word," said L.D. "Gets better every time he tells it."

"Naw, man." Racer lifted his chin. "Looka here, I can prove it." He reached in his pocket, pulled something out, laid it in Clare's upturned palm: a tiny plastic sword. "Frank, man," he whispered reverently.

But the others booed, showered him with pillows again, and then they were all laughing and shouting and Racer was fighting them off. "You're *all* just jealous. But we know what we know, ain't that right, Shoe? Tell 'em, Cowboy."

Cowboy was sitting quietly on the other bed, watching a "Jeopardy!" replay of last year's Tournament of Champions.

"Sorry," said Alex Trebek. "This was a real toughie. What we were looking for was phosphorus, the *light-bearing* element. . . ."

"Cowboy?"

He looked up now, and for just a second he seemed surprised—like an absentminded parent who has temporarily forgotten his children. But then he smiled. "If that's how Racer says it was, then that's how it was," he said.

"There!" cried Racer. "What'd I tell you?"

He looked so triumphant that Clare had to smile, too.

85

They settled down for a while after that, took turns in the bathroom, soaking in the tub. Clare washed her hair three times with the complimentary shampoo. Nothing had ever felt quite as good. The rinsing left an orange stain on the porcelain; her dye job had started to wear off finally, now that the spikes were growing out a little. Maybe at this rate she might actually look human again by Christmas.

"Come on out of there, Fish!" Racer was banging on the door of the bathroom. "It's time!"

"Time for what?" Clare grumbled, turning the knob. "I just want to go to sleep, that's all."

But when she opened the door, the room had changed. Someone had turned off all the lights, lit a pair of candles, and stuck them in the motel water glasses. They were leaning against the rims, dripping little blobs of purple wax on the three-legged table, which had been dragged from its corner and placed in the center of the room, between the two beds. The Monopoly board was set up in the middle.

Racer slapped her on the back. "Told you it was a party, didn't I? Only I didn't say it was for *you!*"

"For me?" Clare was mystified.

"Don't want to be a fish forever, do you?"

"Have a seat," said Cowboy. He gestured toward the room's lone chair—the place of honor, apparently, at the head of the table.

Clare sat. It was just a dumb game, nothing to get excited about; she knew that. So why was her pulse suddenly singing in her ears? "What's up?" she asked, trying to keep her voice light.

"You are," said Cowboy. "Almost, anyway. Six weeks tomorrow you've been with us. Isn't that right?"

"I guess so," said Clare, knowing full well it was. "So what?"

"Tell her, L.D."

Little Dog looked up from his notebook. "It means you're nearly official," he said. "One last test and you're in for good. A regular player."

Racer grinned. "No more little Fishy."

"What kind of test?"

"First things first," said Cowboy. He nodded at Little Dog, who was lining up the playing pieces on Go: horseback rider for Cowboy, car for Racer, thimble for Thimble, little dog, shoe. . . .

"Now you choose," said L.D., and he placed the remaining pieces in the center of the board. Some were missing, Clare was pretty sure; she thought she remembered more—a flatiron maybe? And wasn't there supposed to be some sort of cannon? It had been ages since she had played the real game; they had had one back in Nashville, but every time they got it out, somebody had ended up getting mad. Mama, mostly; she was a terrible loser and Joey always played to win. It was a character flaw, he said, and he never failed to apologize for his combination of greed and luck, but then he would just go right on winning. . . .

The only pieces here now were a miniature wheelbarrow and a tiny top hat. *Just my size,* Joey Morgan would always say, putting it on. *Perfect for a pinhead.* . . .

Clare smiled. "I'll take the hat," she said.

"Done," said Cowboy, handing it to her.

She placed it beside the others on Go.

"Now," said L.D., "only one turn apiece." He checked his notebook. "Shoe first," he said, handing him the dice.

Shoe giggled and rolled a four: three and one. Then he counted out the spaces carefully, silently mouthing the numbers.

"Aww," said Racer. "Income Tax." He patted Shoe's shoulder. "Too bad, my man."

"But what does it mean?" Clare asked. "He can't pay— he don't have any money."

Thimble rolled her eyes. "We told you before, we don't play with *fake* money."

"Just wait," said Cowboy. "Who's next, L.D.?"

"I am," said Little Dog, and rolled a nine.

"Connecticut," Clare said under her breath. With no money and no property cards, obviously he wasn't going to buy anything, but she held her tongue this time.

"Now Racer," said Little Dog, and Racer rolled a two and a four: Oriental Avenue.

Ditto for Thimble, who joined him.

Now there were only the horseback rider and the small silver hat, waiting side by side on Go. It gave Clare a peculiar prickly feeling, seeing the two of them there together, almost touching. *Cut it out*, she told herself. *Are you sick or what?*

Thimble didn't seem to like it much either. "What are we waiting for?" she complained. "Who's next—the new girl?" *The new girl*—Clare was beginning to think she would always be that to Thimble, even if she stayed with the gang a hundred years.

"No," said Little Dog. "Your turn, Cowboy." His voice was respectful.

Cowboy nodded. He picked up the dice, spit on them, rubbed them between his palms, and rolled.

"Eleven!" everybody cried together. They were beaming, Clare noticed, as if he had done something wonderful. "Good roll, Cowboy!"

"Not bad," he admitted. He picked up his piece, moved it to St. Charles Place.

What does it all mean? Clare wanted to scream, but the others were looking at her now, so she stayed cool.

"You're up," said Cowboy, handing her the dice. And she didn't know if it was the brush of his fingers or the uncanny force of the brown eyes, but suddenly she was weak, actually trembling, for crying out loud, though she didn't let on. *What is* wrong *with you?* she asked herself. Taking a deep breath, she shook the dice in her cupped hands, wondered briefly if she should follow Cowboy's example and spit on them, decided that would be pushing it. And then with what she hoped was a casual flick of her wrist, she tossed them to the board.

But her palms were so sweaty now that one die stuck for an instant, then came loose without warning and shot *past* the board, skittering across the flat gray carpet.

Little Dog shook his head disgustedly. "Bad roll," he said.

"Tough luck," said Thimble. There was an unmistakable glint of triumph in her eyes.

Shoe fetched the escapee, placed it carefully on the table.

"It was a one," said Racer. "Plus three makes four. Income Tax again, too bad."

"Off the board doesn't count," said Cowboy. "Roll again."

Thimble frowned. "That's no fair—she blew it already!"

Cowboy ignored her. "Roll again," he ordered.

This time Clare rubbed her hands dry on her shirt before she picked up the dice. Then she rolled a second time: five and five, right in the middle of the Monopoly logo.

"Ten!" Thimble crowed. "Still don't beat Cowboy. You lose, kid."

"No," said Cowboy, placing the hat on the "Just Visiting" part of Jail. "Doubles. Roll again."

'What?" Thimble cried. "I thought L.D. said just one roll apiece!"

"One *turn* apiece," said Cowboy. He looked only at Clare. "Roll again," he repeated.

Clare did as she was told: *another* pair of fives this time.

"Wow!" said Racer. "Free Parking!"

"More doubles," said Little Dog, making some sort of mark in his notebook.

"One more set and you're in jail," Thimble gloated.

"Roll again," said Cowboy.

"Whatever. . . ," said Clare. She shrugged and rolled—

A three.

"Indiana." Thimble sounded disappointed.

But Shoe was giggling again, and Racer cried, "Yes! We have a winner! Way to go, Hat!"

"No," said Little Dog. "She's not official yet, is she, Cowboy? Not until the test is over."

"You're kidding me!" Clare could hardly believe her ears. "It ain't *over*?"

Cowboy smiled. "Not quite," he said.

12

Don't know why—
There's no sun up in the sky;
Stormy weather . . .

THE MELODY sent a shiver down Clare's spine. *Mama's old number.* It had followed her here somehow; for a second she halfway expected to turn around and see the whole band behind her: Jessie James and all the Outlaws, their arms outstretched, reaching for her. . . .

But of course they weren't there; it was only the crippled woman, lying on her cot in the circular glow of the street-light, playing her keyboard. Her frowning companion stood beside her, holding the donations box. Cowboy stopped and said a few words to him, something that made him shrug and shake his head. And then Cowboy nodded at the woman, dropped a couple of bills in the box, and caught up with Clare and the others, pushing up his collar around his neck to shield himself from the wind that was whipping in off the water.

It was no wonder the woman had chosen that particular song tonight. "Hurricane weather," a birdlike old lady was chirping to her companions as the gang brushed past. "I'm from Galveston and I should know. . . ." An exaggeration, surely, but there was *some* kind of nastiness brewing out there, no question, churning the waves into monster shapes, dashing them into wild white spray as they crashed to pieces on the shore. Whistling onto the island then, scattering trash up and down the boardwalk, thrashing the flags outside the convention center; Clare could hear the hollow *pops!* of their flapping, a hundred yards away.

Anything could happen on a night like this. The thought was thrilling and at the same time almost paralyzing; it put lead in Clare's legs as she trudged on toward her trial.

Cowboy was right behind her, watching her; she could feel his brown eyes boring into the back of her skull. She was glad he was there. She still didn't know much about him, next to nothing, really, but somehow it didn't matter anymore. All that mattered was *now*, this very minute. She had said it before, but she hadn't really understood it, had she? *Now* and *now* and *now*. Even the idea of California had begun to lose some of its magic. What would she do when she got there? Travel from town to town, knocking on doors, asking for Joey Morgan? It was a pretty big state, from what she had heard. And she would be alone. . . .

But for *now* she wasn't alone, was she? If she passed this last test, she would never have to be alone again. She would be official, one of the gang. More than a gang—a family. Sure it was, just as much a family as plenty of others she had seen. Had been in, even. Like it said back home in the slogan for DePugh's Fried Chicken: As Good As Most, Better Than Some. A real family. She had never had brothers or sisters, but now she had five. And they were all behind her, rooting for her, not just Cowboy but Racer, too, and Shoe in his own way and even Little Dog and—

"What's *wrong* with you? Can't you hurry?" growled Thimble. "Let's get this over with before it starts to rain."

Well, maybe not *all*.

"I thought you said we shouldn't ever look like we were in a hurry," Clare defended herself, "that the idea was to stay cool, act normal."

"That's once you get *inside* the restaurant, dummy. Nobody cares what you do out here."

"Leave her alone, Thimble." Cowboy's voice was calm, reasonable. "It's her call tonight, remember? We just go along with whatever she decides."

"Even if she decides to get us all soaked?"

"Even then. Her call, got it?"

"Okay, okay. Jeez."

Clare would have liked to gloat, but she wasn't so sure she deserved Cowboy's support. Her call—*Lord*. She hoped to heaven it was the right one. Timing, strategy, every step of the plan was up to her. Even the place they were hitting had been her decision. Well, sort of.

"Anything on the boardwalk within three blocks of Indiana," Little Dog had explained last night, after Clare's silver hat had landed there. "Not bad. Maybe not as much of a choice as if you had landed on Chance, say. Anywhere near a casino would have been up for grabs then. But of course they have all those guards hanging around. Thimble nearly got caught in front of Resorts once, remember that? So maybe you're better off with Indiana, after all. At least it's easier than the railroads, right, Racer?"

"Phew!" he answered, holding his nose. "Old B. & O., man—talk about the pits. Ain't nothing worth hitting in the Amtrak station. Naw, Hatso, Indiana's all right. Better than Boardwalk, if you ask me."

The others had looked shocked. "No way!" Thimble protested. "You roll Boardwalk, the sky's the limit. You can take your pick of any place!"

Racer shook his head. "Naw, man, then you got *too* much to choose from. Helps to narrow it down a little, know what I mean?"

Clare had to agree. Even with a little old three-block limit the selection was dizzying: Brighton Park and the Claridge, Bally's and Madame Edna's and Peanut World and the Garden Terrace Buffet and the All You Can Eat Smorgasbord and Three Brothers From Italy Pizza and Subs and—

"What about Atlantic Jack's?" Little Dog had suggested, checking some list in his notebook. "We've never hit that before."

The blood went charging to Clare's cheeks. "No," she said, more loudly than necessary. Then "No way" in a smaller voice.

"Why not?" Thimble was suddenly interested. "Were you ever inside?"

Clare shrugged. She kept her face down, started pushing the little hat around the board. "I don't know," she muttered. "Once, maybe."

"Might want to think about it then," said Little Dog. "Always helps to know the layout ahead of time."

Clare started to shake her head, but then Racer had to

open his mouth: "Atlantic Jack's—that's the hot-dog man, right? Old dude that don't pay attention to nothing, all the time trotting down them stairs to his basement."

"Who cares?" Clare muttered. She could see the old man still, coming through that door, the one marked No Admittance, carrying that stupid stack of letters—*Dear Joey, please Joey*—ugh. Made her sick to her stomach still just to think of it. But Racer just rattled right on:

"Sure, that's the one. Me and Shoe, we figure he's hiding something down there, don't we? Like maybe he's one of them old dudes that don't trust banks, got to keep all his money tied up in a pillowcase, you know how they do? Tried to sneak down there one time, Shoe and me, see for ourselfs. Nothing to it at first, door wasn't even locked. But then the old man, I guess he keeps an eye on it someway, he comes after us before we're halfway down. 'Can I help you, gentlemen?' he says, real polite. 'We was only looking for the rest room,' I say. 'One door over,' he tells us, and that's the end of it. Not much of a talker, old Atlantic Jack. Durn near quiet as the Shoe." Racer gave his friend an affectionate poke in the ribs.

"Maybe he's dealing drugs," Thimble suggested.

"Naw, man, he ain't the type. 'Course, you never know. Can't see in them little windows. He's got 'em all frosted up, know what I mean? Could be he's nuts, keeping him some old dead lady like in that *Psycho* movie. Got to watch out for them quiet dudes. They're gonna *getcha* when you ain't looking." Racer grabbed Clare around the waist, causing her to jump and Shoe to double over with hysterics; he had to make an emergency run to the bathroom to get over them.

Clare didn't think it was all that funny. "Cut it *out*, Racer."

"Aw, Hatso, what's the matter? Don'tchoo wanna play no more?"

Clare sighed. "Just forget it," she said.

But Thimble was smiling. "I'll tell you what's the matter with her. She's scared. Ain't that right, kid? Something about that place has you spooked."

Clare's head jerked up. "It don't either," she said, glowering. "I just—just don't like it, that's all."

Thimble was one of those people who can move a single eyebrow at a time. The left one shot up now; it made her look downright fiendish. "Oh, yeah?" she said. "Why?"

Clare hesitated. It wasn't just a question of *like*; she *hated* Atlantic Jack's, hated every stupid thing about it—which for some reason she could remember with astounding clarity: the crazy kids' toys and those weird model planes and the music from the jukebox and the smell of mustard. Ever since that day even the slightest whiff of the stuff could make her queasy. And the old man with the mustache and the mismatched eyes—she hated him most of all—that old man who had stood there stammering and clearing his stupid throat, trying to tell her Joey Morgan wasn't there. . . .

"No reason," she said, looking at her fingernails; they were filthy, she noted absently, even after half an hour in the tub. "It just stinks, that's all."

"Then hit it," said Thimble. "That's reason enough."

"What?"

"She's got a point," said Little Dog. "No sense hitting places you like. Can't go back for months sometimes—gotta wait till things cool down a little. Might as well pick a spot you won't miss."

"There you go, Hatso." Racer slapped her back. "Let's

do it, man. Something big in the basement, I'm telling you."

It was all too confusing. Maybe they were right; if you hate it, hit it. Maybe this was the one place in Atlantic City that *deserved* to be hit. . . .

Good Lord, said that voice inside her—the one that grew fainter every day. *If Father Cavanaugh could only hear you now*. Not that it really mattered, all that mashed potato about her immortal soul—if she even had one anymore. Still, the idea made her sick someway. She shook her head. "No," she said. "I don't think so."

"Told you," said Thimble. "She's scared."

"I am *not*," Clare shot back.

"So prove it," said Thimble.

"She doesn't have to prove anything." Cowboy hadn't taken part in the discussion up till now; he had just sat back and listened, his fingertips pressed together, forming a sort of Christmas tree. "Except what she wants to prove," he added quietly. He looked at Clare. "Forget Thimble. Forget everybody. It's your call."

No one spoke for a minute. It seemed to Clare that the whole world was leaning in, waiting for her decision.

"Well," she began; she was going to ask Little Dog to read over that list in his notebook once more. There had been one or two places that had sounded all right—

And then Thimble sneered. Just a tiny sneer—an infinitesimal flare of a nostril, the faintest curl of a lip.

But it worked.

"Okay," Clare said through clenched teeth. "Atlantic Jack's. Who cares, anyhow?"

□ □ □

Now came the thunder.

They arrived just as it began—great booming peals of it, splitting the night apart: one Mississippi, two Mississippi, *boom-cracka-BOOM!*

Good grief, thought Clare. *Sound effects.*

She was huddled with the others just under the outside overhang of the mall entrance, about fifty boardwalk yards south plus a stone's throw across to the hot-dog joint. "All right," she said, trying to sound as if she knew what she was doing, "y'all know the plan?"

A nod from Cowboy, smothered giggles from Shoe.

"No sweat," said Racer.

"Check," said Little Dog.

Thimble rolled her eyes. "Let's just *do* it," she said.

"Okay, then." Clare took a deep breath. "First group, move out."

Racer and Shoe grinned and saluted, sauntered off together.

The sound of the jukebox drifted out as they opened the door, then stopped abruptly as the door swung shut. Through the lighted window Clare could see the guys slide into a booth, smile at a skinny waitress who handed them a pair of menus. So far, so good.

"Now us," she said to Thimble, when the five prearranged minutes had crawled by. Not that Thimble was exactly her idea of a perfect partner; there just hadn't been much of a choice, really. Dividing up was crucial to the plan, Shoe always had to be with Racer, and somehow Clare couldn't stand the thought of Thimble sitting alone with Cowboy tonight. Still, she wouldn't have dared choose him for herself. . . .

Thimble didn't seem exactly overjoyed with the arrangement either. She didn't wait even five seconds for Clare but started off across the boardwalk immediately, swinging her hips more than anyone needed to; you could practically see the contempt in her backside. "Five minutes," Clare threw over her shoulder to Cowboy and Little Dog, and then she ran to catch up.

The restaurant was just as she remembered it—only even junkier, if that was possible—cluttered with every imaginable oddity. Laurel and Hardy were still there, and the soda wheel and the toy train and the man with the beard of bees and a couple of pictures she hadn't noticed before: a bride and groom getting married on a roller coaster, a painter balancing on one foot atop the Eiffel Tower—"A Light Heart Lives Long" said the caption underneath that one. *Right*, thought Clare. *How about a light brain?* She lifted her eyes to the ceiling. Yep, the planes were still there, too. Were there even more now? Thousands of them, it seemed to her tonight, wave after wave after wave of wings—

"Don't stare," said Thimble, giving her a little shove. "It makes you look like a jerk."

"I wasn't staring," Clare whispered icily, though of course she had been. She summoned up what she hoped was a withering look, crossed to a corner table, and pulled out a chair. Thimble followed. Not sheepishly or anything, but at least she followed.

It was only a half hour till closing time, but the place was still fairly well packed. That was good; easier to be invisible in a crowd. Clare glanced across the room at Racer and Shoe, who didn't appear to be sticking out any more than usual, except that Racer was pouring ketchup in his water glass and Shoe had that look on his face that meant he might break out in giggles at any minute. Clare tried narrowing her eyes sternly at him, but she couldn't really tell if he got the message. Or saw her, even. *Come on, y'all, shape up!* she wanted to holler. *Ain't no time to be kidding around!* But just then Santiago crossed to her table, handed menus to her and Thimble, and walked away without giving her even a second glance, though Clare's heart was pounding so loudly that she was sure he would turn around. "What *is* that noise?" he would say, and then he was bound to recognize her. . . .

He didn't. Still, Clare felt as if she had barely escaped disaster, although she was pretty sure she didn't look the same as she had that other time, without the green heels or *quite* the same orange hair. And for once she had left off the blue sunglasses, too, just to be on the safe side, though she felt almost naked without them. You just never knew about adults, was the thing; sometimes they looked right through you and sometimes they could pick you out of a whole stadium full of people. Which was why she had been hoping for the skinny waitress, too. . . .

But Santiago was back behind the counter now and the old man was working the grill, probably couldn't even see her through the smoke, so it looked as if she were safe.

She pretended to study the menu, but all the time her eyes were peering over the top: more than half the tables filled with customers, a couple of booths empty next to Racer and Shoe, the skinny waitress taking a tray to a pair of lovers—a guy with bad skin and a sweet-looking girl with a nubby brown sweater pulled over her narrow shoulders. Nothing Clare couldn't handle. And in the back of the room, there between the rest rooms and a spiraling metal staircase that must lead to the upper stories—living quarters maybe?—was the door to the basement. No Admittance, it still announced in threatening black letters, but it was a little late to be worrying about that now.

"It's too risky," Little Dog had said when he heard her plan, though it was the best she had been able to come up with on such short notice. "No telling what's down there. Racer's just running his mouth. Besides, how can you be sure that door won't be locked?"

"No sweat, man," Racer had offered. "I could go to the rest room, check out the knob on my way. Anybody sees me, I can always say I had the wrong door."

He was returning from his mission now, slipping back into his booth across from Shoe and grinning like that old canary-swallowing cat, so that Clare knew, even before he nodded and gave her the thumbs-up signal, that everything was proceeding as planned. She nodded back and tried to look pleased, but the truth was her heart was sinking. This was it, then; there would be no excuses.

Thimble seemed to understand somehow. "No turning back now, huh, kid?" she whispered. And for an instant Clare wasn't sure—was she being her usual snotty self, or was there just the slightest hint of sympathy in her eyes? Couldn't be, could there? *Nah, no way.*

Thunder rumbled again, rattling the windows. Clare looked up just in time to see the front door swinging open. Cowboy and Little Dog ambled inside, chose a table next to the model train. *Good work, guys.* Now they had the whole room covered.

Santiago was back. "Are you ladies ready to order?" he asked. "I don't like to rush you, but our closing time is soon. And you want to be at home before this storm gets to breaking."

KABOOM-BA-BOOM! went the thunder, and with

that the electricity faltered. "Ooooh," the customers moaned softly, then laughed, "Aah, ha, ha!" when it flickered back on, just as the first drops of rain began to pelt against the windows. Santiago chuckled. "Too late," he said. "She's broke already. So, you order now?"

"Coupla dogs all the way," said Thimble. "And fries and a root beer."

"Same for me," Clare murmured, keeping her face well covered with the menu.

"Coming right up," said Santiago, moving away.

Clare started breathing again, looked over at Racer and Shoe. They had got their food already and were eating happily, stopping every now and then to gaze at the model planes overhead or to blow the papers from their straws at each other. *Good grief, guys, are you paying attention? It's almost time!* Little Dog, now, he knew how to act, sitting there imitating Cowboy's every move. Not that he was *entirely* successful; Clare could see his eyes darting nervously about, while Cowboy took his time over the menu, studying every detail. It was the difference between trying to be cool and being cool without trying. . . .

"There you are, ladies. Pretty speedy service, hey? Anything else you need, just be whistling."

Almost time now, almost time—

Cowboy was looking at her, a question in his eyes. She frowned a little, gave him an almost imperceptible shake of her head. *Not yet, not quite yet.* Better wait just a minute or two, try to eat something maybe; that was the natural thing to do. No way she could have touched the hot dogs, though Thimble wasn't having any trouble with hers, she noticed. Maybe just a couple of fries; that wouldn't kill her, would it?

102

One potato, two potato, three potato, four. Thimble chewed away steadily, but Clare's throat was so tight that even the root beer was having trouble getting through. *Now?* Racer was looking her way this time. *Be ready,* she tried to tell him with her eyes, *we're nearly there. . . .*

The sweet-faced girl and her boyfriend got up, started to peer doubtfully out the window at the sheets of rain blowing down the boardwalk. For the first time Clare noticed an old cuckoo clock hanging on the wall above a sign that read TIME AND TIDE WAIT FOR NO MAN. The clock had stopped at midnight—or was it noon?—who knew how long ago. Behind the counter, Santiago was glancing at his own wristwatch and frowning a little; must be closing time by now, surely.

Five potato, six potato, seven potato—no! She couldn't go through with it after all. It was too late; the right minute had passed and now her chance was gone, finished. *So long, sucker; see you in the funny papers—*

Now? the brown eyes were asking once more, or not asking, exactly—demanding was more like it. Clare swallowed hard. The small lump of french fry felt like a golf ball. *Lord, help me,* she thought, and nodded.

Now.

Thimble reached in her lap, got something out of her purse, slid it under her napkin. "Okay," she whispered to Clare, who stood up and began walking across the room, stopping to speak to the skinny waitress, who was passing another table: "Excuse me, could you tell me where the rest room is?"

"Sure—second door on your right, just beyond those stairs there."

"Thank you," said Clare, continuing on her way.

103

And then a dozen things happened all together:

Thimble gave a bloodcurdling yell, prompting every head in the room to turn toward her at once. And then Racer began to yell, too, so they all snapped over in that direction. Meanwhile Shoe stood up on his chair and commenced a kind of maniacal rain dance, waving his arms wildly and lifting them heavenward, and at the same time Little Dog rose suddenly, knocking over his loaded table, which came crashing down at Cowboy's feet just as Clare reached the other side of the room and opened not the restroom door (clearly marked Ladies) but the forbidden one beside it.

And that should have been the end of everything, but just then there was a white-hot flash of lightning, so close this time that Clare could smell a sort of burning odor, as if it had scorched the very air, and almost instantaneously the electric lights in the restaurant began to falter again, sputtering back to life for a split second and then dying altogether, while in the same heartbeat there came a horrific ear-shattering noise, the most awful thunder yet: *CRRRAC-CCKKKAACRAAACKKKAAABBBOOOOMMMMM!!!!!* Which caused Clare to panic somehow and lurch in exactly the wrong direction, so that even as the door swung shut behind her, she lost her footing and went hurtling down the cellar stairs.

Shoot, she thought as she tumbled head over heels. *This ain't—what I had—in mind.* Some sort of bombshell exploded inside her brain then; there was a searing burst of pain, and suddenly she was watching what appeared to be a fireworks display on one of those giant-screened televisions: Roman candles and whistling chasers and multicolored bottle rockets going off all at once—*BAM! POW! FIZZLE! POP!*

No way, she thought. *Death by Looney Tunes.*

And then the screen went black.

13

WHEN SHE OPENED her eyes, she didn't know where she was. Someplace dark, horribly dark, the only light a pitiful glimmer coming from two frosted windows far above her. Small horizontal windows, they were, oddly distant from the cold, damp floor where she found herself lying.

I'm dreaming, she told herself. *I'll turn over and this will be gone, changed into another dream. A better dream.*

But when she tried to move, a fiery, double-fisted jolt of pain went tearing through her, slamming into her left arm, shooting up over her right eye. It cleared her head somehow, burned its way through the fog in her brain.

And suddenly she remembered. All of it. *Good Lord, what a mess.* How long had she been lying here anyway? What had happened to the others? Were they still upstairs playing lunatic, or had they managed to slip outside before the commotion died down, waiting for her back on Baltic as planned?

She listened for the sound of footsteps in the room overhead, but there were none—not a peep anywhere but the noise of the rain, beating down like a jillion tiny buffalo hooves on the boardwalk, just outside the frosted windows. That and her own blood, thrumming in her ears.

Panic seized her. Was she all alone, then? Closed up in the old guy's basement with—*with what?* Some dead lady, like Racer had said? She strained her eyes, tried to peer through the darkness. Huge, eerie shapes loomed everywhere, misshapen shadows that were all the more terrible because they made no sense. They didn't look like anything she had ever seen before—nothing like what you'd expect to find in a cellar. What *would* you expect to find in a cellar anyway? What was it Racer had gone on about? Pillowcases filled with hundred-dollar bills just lying around waiting to be lifted? Lord, it all seemed so *stupid* now—

The plan. *Her* plan—what a joke that was; what a stinker of a plan it had been! She could see it all so clearly, lying here in the dark; why not last night, before it was too late? What in the *world* had she been thinking?

And yet it had seemed reasonable enough at the time— the first part anyway—when Racer had suggested it to her. He had borrowed it from one of his everlasting movies:

"*Victor/Victoria*, man—ain't you ever seen that one? Where old Julie Andrews puts a roach in her food so she won't have to pay for it? Only it gets away and climbs up some fat lady's leg and pretty soon she's screaming *her* head off? And then first thing you know, everybody else is screaming, too, and the whole place goes crazy, so Julie and old what's his name, Robert Preston, they just sneak right out the front door, no problem. Aw, it's great, man—been meaning to use it myself, but you're the one gotta make good this time. So it's a present, how you like that? I give it to you for free."

Thanks, pal.

But she really couldn't complain, because that part of the plan had actually worked out pretty well—at least as far as she knew. The whole point being to create a diversion, to stir up such a fuss that the old man and everybody else would be too busy looking at the show to notice her slipping through the basement door. And then the rest of the scheme was all hers, so she couldn't blame anyone but herself for the way it had turned out. For the fact that she was lying here like a sack of bruised potatoes, alone in the dark—dark so thick she could almost feel its hairy arms closing about her, smell its sour black peanut breath close in her face—

Stop it! she ordered herself. *What are you, a crybaby?*

Oh, no, nobody's fault but hers. . . .

The *idea* had been for her to take her time while all the hollering was going on in the room upstairs, have a look around the cellar, just on the outside chance that Racer was right and there really was something worth picking up down there. But even if there wasn't, it was no big deal; she would just lie low until the restaurant cleared out for the night, then slide back upstairs when she was sure it was safe and hit the cash register—which was one of those old-fashioned ones, naturally, like all the rest of the junk in the place. She ought to be able to jimmy it with just a pocketknife and the small flat-head screwdriver that Little Dog had taught her to use. And even if *that* didn't work out—if the register was too tough to crack after all—there was bound to be something she could lift, *something* in all that trash that would be a consolation prize at least. The toy train, maybe, or a couple of those model planes; they might be worth a few bucks to some ice-cream-licking tourist kid. Not that money was the whole point of the test—

"Oh, no," Little Dog had explained when she asked. "Not the *whole* point. First you get scored on the plan itself—its all-around excellence, I mean, and then on how daring it is, and of course there's the execution. That's the main thing."

Still, she had had high hopes about the money. That one night in the motel had made her want more; maybe she would score really big, make enough to keep them all in olives and mattresses for a week. *Two* weeks maybe.

Oh, it hadn't been such a *terrible* plan, had it? Not so terrible, after all. Who knew, maybe it might even have worked, if she hadn't fallen on her stupid head. Maybe she might have actually pulled it off—grabbed whatever she could, waited till the coast was clear, then simply unlocked the front door and waltzed outside, or broken a window if she had to, if you needed a key, say. And then by this time she'd already be back at the Baltic house, laughing with Shoe at how easy it had been, listening to Racer make his part ten times better than it really was. Watching the envy in Thimble's eyes, the quiet approval in Cowboy's—

The thought made her throat ache. She had wanted to make him proud. . . .

A single tear welled up in her swollen right eye, rolled sideways down her temple. What would he think of her now? What *could* he think but the truth—that she was a big clumsy bozo with balance like the *Titanic's*, a bumbling joke not worth all his trouble. That it turned out Thimble had been right about her all along. Oh, wouldn't Thimble have a good laugh now?

The picture was so infuriating—old Fuzz-head laughing—that for a minute Clare forgot to be miserable. She wiped her nose with the back of her good hand, dabbed roughly at the wet trail the tear had left. *All right, girl,* now *what? You still got a head—a little mashed in on one side maybe, but it's better than nothing, so use it, do you hear me? You can't just keep lying here. No telling what time it is already. . . .*

She checked herself for injuries first, using her right arm, moving her hand gingerly over the egg-shaped welt above her eye. It was sticky to the touch; she must have caught it on a stair corner on her way down, got some pretty good bleeding going on there. But it seemed to have clotted up all right; that was lucky, anyway. *Wouldn't be much fun to bleed to death alone in the dark, would it?* The thought was too awful to dwell on; she pushed it away, moved her hand down to the injured arm.

Good Lord in heaven—the pain was so excruciating that it was all she could do to keep from hollering. She waited another minute to get her breath back, and then she gritted her teeth and continued her investigation. Well, that was peculiar; the arm felt as if it had got screwed on backward somehow—it was twisted all catawampus at the shoulder. But the worst pain was lower down, from the elbow clear through to the wrist. "Wiggle your fingers," the teachers would always say when somebody had a fall in the school yard; Clare tried that now, but the pain was so sharp it brought tears to her eyes, and she gave it up right away. *Shoot.* There was something broken in there, all right. Still, it could have been worse; at least she wasn't left-handed. And her legs seemed to be all right, so she could move, as long as she took it easy. That was the main thing; if she could move, maybe she could get out of this mess.

110

Slowly, carefully, so as not to intensify the throbbing in her head, the stabbing in her arm, she pulled herself up to a sitting position. She had to rest for a moment there, wait for her head to stop swimming so, and then, using the wall as support, she slid along it, an inch at a time, until she was on her feet. A breath, and then with her right hand she groped uncertainly in the blackness until her fingers touched the stair railing. This she grasped with all her strength, and hanging on for dear life, she began the long haul back up the stairs.

Slow, now, sister. Take it easy. We ain't about to make that trip again. . . . She had to stop and rest on each step, fight off the waves of dizziness and nausea that kept sweeping over her, threatening to stop her altogether. But she wouldn't let them; again and again she steadied herself, set her jaw against the pain, and kept climbing. *Easy, I said, one foot up and then the other. There you go now, that's the way—*

Suddenly she froze. Footsteps. Up there somewhere beyond the closed door, ringing strangely—on the winding metal staircase maybe? Yes, she was sure of it; there they were again, descending into the dining room now, crossing near the counter to the—to the kitchen maybe? *Please, whoever you are, go to the kitchen, stay in the kitchen! You're just hungry, right? Coming down for a little snack?*

But the footsteps only paused for a moment, then began again, *tap, tap, tapping* across the wooden floor, not loud but solid, deliberate. . . . Getting *louder* now? Coming closer, coming—

This way!

Hide! Got to hide—got to get away. But where?

Frantically Clare turned and fled down the stairs into

the darkness below, into whatever this vast black room was, its weird shapes looming like giants with their arms open wide, waiting to catch her.

Hide! Quick—get away, get away!

There was a flash of lightning, too brief to be of any use to her; the shapes around her were still meaningless, menacing. Now a distant rumbling, barely audible above the din of raindrops. The thunder was moving away, then, but all the time the footsteps were coming closer, closer. . . .

Got to hide, got to get away, must be somewhere *to hide—*

The door was opening up above at the head of the stairs; she could hear its hinges squeaking. No time left—none at all. If only she could see! Her left arm still hung uselessly at her side, but her right was stretched before her like a lopsided sleepwalker's as she tried to feel her way. Here was something, now—something smooth and cold that seemed to be attached to some sort of—*what?* A table maybe? That was better than nothing. She would try to crawl under it; maybe she would be safe there. . . .

But in her haste and blindness she knocked over something beside it—some awful metal something that fell to the floor with a horrible clattering just as the light was switched on.

Silence then. That deafening silence that can come only after the worst kind of racket. Dead still, except for the howling of the wind, the drumming of the rain. And then—

"Who's there?"

It was the old man's voice.

Crouched on the floor, wedged between the table and

some hard object she couldn't make out, Clare covered her head with her arm, closed her eyes tight. She knew it was stupid, like some little kid who thinks if she can't see, no one can see her. But she couldn't help it.

"I said who's down there? I'll give you till the count of five. One . . ."

This ain't real, she told herself. *It's the worst nightmare you ever had, that's all, worse than the worst. And in a minute you're going to wake up, and you'll tell Racer about it, and he'll laugh and laugh—*

"Two . . ."

Think, think, got to think. Can't run—nowhere to hide. What if he's got a gun? What if he comes down and starts blasting away?

"Three . . ."

Got to give yourself up, tell him the truth, ain't no other way, is there? Not the whole truth, just a part of it—enough to get by, enough to get away—

"Four . . ."

"Stop! Don't shoot! It was just an accident. I was trying to find the rest room, and I must have opened the wrong door." The words stumbled over one another in their haste to get out of her mouth, which felt furry somehow, coated with wool. She tried to shout them as she crawled out from under the table, pulled herself painfully to her feet, but the noise of her own voice set her head pounding worse than ever, so she had to continue in a more halting fashion: "And then I—I tripped somehow. I lost my balance, and I fell down the stairs, and I guess—I guess I must have blacked out—"

She broke off all at once. Her eyes were open now, but

the room was spinning, and what she saw as it spun past was so astonishing that she decided she must be dreaming after all.

Because for just a second there she could have sworn that her hiding place wasn't a table at all, but the wing of an enormous airplane.

14

"IT'S A BEAUTIFUL DAY in the Neighborhood" sounded sweetly from the television across the hall.

You gotta be kidding me, thought Clare.

This time when she opened her eyes she knew exactly where she was. And she wanted out.

It was a small yellow room, so glaringly yellow it made her long for the blue sunglasses. A pair of cartwheeling clowns grinned at her from a picture frame on one wall. On another several pigs were dancing. The kiddie ward, for crying out loud—didn't they know she was too old to be stuck in a place like this?

Not that she had told them her age—or anything else, for that matter. "Call me Hat" was all she would say last night to the curly-headed nurse when she asked her name for the twenty-seventh time.

"Cat?" The nurse had leaned in close. Her breath

smelled of garlic. "Did you say Cat, honey? For Catherine? Or Kathleen?"

"Hat," Clare had muttered. The garlic was making her feel even sicker than she already was. "For Monopoly."

"Do you think she's delirious?" the old man had asked. He had been the one the word was closer to fitting, in Clare's opinion. A wreck was what he was—practically frantic with worry.

But the nurse had only sighed, scribbled something in a folder. "Not delirious," she said. "Just stubborn. We'll try again in the morning."

Go ahead, try, thought Clare. *Ain't no way y'all are gonna get me to talk.*

She frowned now at the dancing pigs. Oh, she'd be out of here like a shot if they hadn't got her all strapped in— the broken arm set and encased in a monstrous white cast, then hung up beside her in a weird sling contraption that made it look as if it weren't even a part of her anymore, some alien being, connected only by a throbbing rope of pain. And then on the other side they had her hooked up to some stupid tube; they had shoved it in her good arm when she hadn't been able to stop throwing up for a while there. That had been a barrel of laughs.

"Not an unusual reaction to a concussion," the doctor told the old man, though Clare was fairly certain it was only the nurse's garlic breath that had finally got to her. "Probably not serious, but we'll have to keep her under observation for a few days, just to make sure she stays perfectly still."

Clare had panicked. "I ca-cat—stay here," she had mumbled, shaking her head. She couldn't seem to make herself clear; by this time they had given her some kind of shot that had thickened her tongue, made her lips feel the way they do after a trip to the dentist—five times their normal size. But the old man had understood her somehow.

"It's all right, miss. Don't you worry. Just rest now, won't you? We'll take care of everything else." And then he had shaken his own head and added apologetically, "If I hadn't left that door unlocked, you wouldn't be in this fix."

Which was only a *piece* of the truth, of course, but she couldn't very well tell *him* that. Still, even in her hurting, half-crazed state, there was a part of her that had cringed when he said it. *Just shut up!* she wanted to scream at him. *What are you doing, trying to get sued? Ain't you ever watched those lawyer ads on television? "Larry Lowlife got me fifty thousand dollars for* my *accident. . . ." Come on, man—there are* vultures *out there!*

But the old man apparently had no sense whatsoever, because he had stayed beside her through the whole vomity mess, mumbling an odd mixture of contrition and encouragement: "There now, miss, you're going to be all right, don't you worry. I'm so sorry about all this, miss. . . ." And then he had run out of words and just *stood* there, looking so stricken, so absolutely wretched that she almost felt sorry for *him*, for crying out loud.

Still, she had kept it to herself—had kept everything to herself—so far at least. *Just like old Shoe, right? If he can do it, then so can I*, she thought. It was only for a little while, anyway; just until she rested up a bit more. Then when they unhooked this stupid tube, she'd unstrap the other arm and be gone—*zip! Whip!* Oh, wouldn't she, though? She had to get back to the others; what in the world must they be thinking?

□ □ □

"Well, well—Sleeping Beauty is awake, is she?" Another nurse—not the curly-headed one but a tall, cheerful-looking woman—came bustling in now. "Feeling better this afternoon?"

"Afternoon?"

"Oh, yes, it's past two already," said the nurse, popping a thermometer under Clare's tongue. "The painkillers had you pretty well knocked out all morning. Let's just see what this says, shall we? And then we're going to get you all cleaned up and squared away. You have two visitors waiting outside."

Cowboy, thought Clare, a little surge of gladness pushing through her. *Cowboy and Little Dog maybe?* They had found her somehow, had gone back to the restaurant and asked around when she didn't show up at the Baltic house. Had risked everything, chanced being recognized—getting turned in to the cops, even—all for her sake—

"The older one's been here all morning," the nurse went on, taking out the thermometer and holding it up to the light. "Asks about you every five minutes. 'Let her rest,' I keep telling him. 'She's had a tough night.' "

It *was* Cowboy, then! He hadn't given up on her, in spite of everything. And now he had come to take her away. . . .

"Do you think you could make it to the bathroom?" the nurse was asking now. "Or would you prefer the bedpan?"

Yuck, thought Clare. "I can make it," she said. No way she was using a bedpan with Cowboy right outside.

"You're the boss," said the nurse, and then she freed the good arm, unstrapped the bad one—Clare gritted her teeth until that was over—and helped Clare to her feet.

118

"Whoa," she said as the world started spinning again.

"Still a little dizzy?" the nurse asked.

"Just a little," Clare admitted.

"Well, that's no surprise with a bump like yours! Just lean on me, honey. It'll pass in a second."

Sure enough, it did, and then Clare nodded to the nurse, who helped her to the bathroom. "Want me to stay?" she asked, but Clare shook her head. "Okay, but I'll be right outside. Just shout if you need me."

And then she closed the door, and Clare turned around, and for a second there she almost *did* shout—not out of pain or dizziness, but because she had caught a glimpse of herself in the bathroom mirror.

Good Lord. The welt over her right eye had swollen to monstrous proportions. It was no longer egg-sized; egg*plant* was more like it—a big fat eggplant of a lump, covered with an enormous white bandage. Which combined with the cast on her arm made her look like a character in one of those old horror movies—Frankenstein's freak, maybe, or The Mummy, oh, yeah, that was the guy. And then whoever had fixed her up had tried to leave her with the use of her right eye, but they might have saved themselves the trouble; it was swollen almost completely shut anyhow, and the little bit that showed was so gross-looking it made Clare want to start gagging again. The other eye had swollen and pinked up, too—just to get in on the fun, she supposed— and both of them were rimmed in horrible disaster colors: not black eyes, exactly—purple-green-red-pinkish-blue eyes was what they were. *Great.* And she had thought she was bad-looking *before*! How could she let Cowboy see her like this?

She lifted a matted strand of hair—which wasn't just

orange anymore but Halloween colored, laced with clumps of dried black blood—and without warning a crazy memory flashed in her mind: Mrs. Gilbert Fontaine back home, leading the Prayer of the Faithful at church two Easters ago. Old prissy Mrs. Fontaine, dolled up fit to kill and too vain to wear her reading glasses. "Let us pray," she had intoned in her grandest Altar Society manner, "for the poor, the hungry, and the victims of homeliness."

That's you, Clare told herself, staring forlornly at the mess in the mirror. *You're a victim of homeliness.* For some reason it made her feel like laughing and crying at the same time, remembering that day, remembering how tickled she and Joey had got, how they had made the whole pew shake, trying to hold in their laughter. Mama had looked bullets at them, wouldn't even take their hands at the "Peace be with you," until she had caught the disease, too, somehow. And then all three of them were biting the insides of their mouths and digging their fingernails into the palms of their hands, but none of it did any good; they were laughing so hard it hurt.

Suddenly Clare wanted her mother. Not with her head; it came from some other part of her, this wanting, something deeper—her gallbladder maybe. It made no sense, she knew that. But for some stupid reason, sitting here looking like warmed-over death on this cold toilet seat in this bathroom reeking of hospital disinfectant, she wanted her more than she had ever wanted anyone in her whole life. Not Sid, of course; she didn't want *him*. Just Mama, the way she could be sometimes when she was in a good mood, the way she used to be. Like in the old days, when Clare was little, when she got sick and Mama would take care of her, let her stay home from school if she wanted to, fix her chicken noodle soup from a can, with little pieces of saltines crumbled up and getting all mushy inside. . . . Oh, if it hadn't been for Mama's drinking, maybe they would have been okay. If it hadn't been for Sid and his greasy fingers—

"You all right in there, honey?"

"Yes, ma'am, just a minute."

Clare blew her nose on a rough half tissue from the stainless-steel dispenser. *What's wrong with you?* she scolded herself. *That's right, see if you can puff up your eyes a little more, why don't you? They ain't quite ugly enough yet. Trying to scare Cowboy off—is that the idea?*

She finished up in the bathroom, tidying herself as best she could with a one-handed go at soap and water and a comb she found in the drawer by the sink. Then she made her way back to the other room, where the nurse helped her get all propped up and strapped in the bed again.

"All right, honey," she said, when Clare was settled, "you ready for company?"

"Ready," said Clare.

"You're looking *much* better," the nurse lied, giving her an encouraging little pat. She walked over to the door. "You can come in now," she said, swinging it open. "But try not to tire her out too much just yet."

"We understand," said a voice Clare only half remembered—not Cowboy's, after all.

No, she saw with a stab of disappointment, it wasn't Cowboy. Just the old man again.

"Hello, Miss Caldwell," he said, his face still wreathed in worry lines. *Shoot.* He had remembered her name, then. "I hope you're feeling—a bit better today," he went on hesitantly; he was still standing in the middle of the doorway, holding a huge bouquet of balloons that blocked Clare's view of everything else. *Perfect,* she thought. *They'll look right at home with the three little piggies.* And then he stepped inside with the balloons, and Clare looked behind him, expecting to see old what's his name maybe—that other guy from the hot-dog joint—Santiago, that was it.

But it wasn't Santiago.

"Hello, Clare Frances," said the red-haired man.

15

SHE WOULD have screamed if she could have made a sound. As it was, terror clogged her throat, closed it completely.

The red-haired man was smiling. "So tell us, how are you? I hear last night was pretty rocky."

Clare didn't—couldn't—answer.

"This is Mr. Griffey, Miss Caldwell," said the old man. He looked perfectly miserable for some reason, as if every word were a trial. But apparently he felt obligated to overcome his shyness and smooth things over, even if it killed him. "He's from the—with—one of the agencies here—" The old man broke off there, then cleared his throat and blundered on doggedly: "He's here to help you. To help us, that is—help us get things sorted out."

"What things?" Clare managed with a mighty effort, doing her best to keep the panic out of her tone. They knew her name; just how much more did they know?

Plenty, it seemed.

"We've just been talking with your mother," said Griffey. (No way Clare would ever call him "Mister" anything.) "She's pretty—upset, I'm afraid. She's been worried about you."

Clare shrugged to cover her trembling. It was all over, then; Mama knew everything. And now she would come for her; now Clare would have to go back. How had they figured it out? The old man had recognized her, of course; that had been their first clue. But it wouldn't have been enough by itself, would it? Surely not, not without something more, something like—

The letter. It came to her very clearly all at once—Joey's letter with the five-dollar bill inside. She had been hiding it in her underwear ever since the day that Shoe had tried to take it, but they must have found it when they undressed her, while she was knocked out last night. *Good Lord,* she asked herself disgustedly, *did you have to make it so easy for them?*

She swallowed hard. "Is she—is she coming, then?" Maybe it wasn't so terrible, really; it was even a relief in a way, after all these weeks of running. At least now the chase was over. Mama would be furious, sure, but Clare was used to that; she could stand that if only—she hardly dared to hope, but still it was *possible*—if only Sid wasn't there anymore. The others had always left eventually; why not him? And then it would be just the two of them again, the way it was when she was little. Maybe there would even be chicken noodle soup—

But why wasn't anybody answering? Griffey and the old man were just standing there, looking at each other, so

Clare repeated herself; maybe they hadn't heard her the first time: "She's coming, ain't she?"

"No," said Griffey. "She's not coming, Clare."

The old man cleared his throat again, added hastily, "Not—not right away, Miss Caldwell. I'm sure she wants to, but it seems she has—ah, pressing business obligations just now. . . ."

It was as if Mama had reached across five states and struck her full in the face. *Business obligations?* Clare knew what that meant—some two-bit gig with the Outlaws, that was all, something she'd ditch in a heartbeat for half an excuse. Maybe not to pick up her only daughter in the hospital; oh, no, she couldn't possibly tear herself away just for that. But for anything *really* important—her beauty operator's second cousin's wedding or a touch of laryngitis or even a hangover, for pete's sake. In the middle of a hangover, that was probably when they had called her; sure it was—just after noon, why, that was early morning to Jessie James. And she was mad, that's what—not "pretty upset," no, sir—she was fire-breathing, nail-spitting, fist-flying mad; mornings were never any time to hit her with bad news. Mad about the forty-four bucks, mad about being fooled, mad about anything Clare had ever done wrong in all her twelve years, nine months, and twenty-odd days. Oh, she could hear her hollering all the way from Nashville: *You just tell that little thief I've had it with her, do you hear me? If she wants to go running after her precious Joey Morgan, well, then, let her. Let him listen to her lies, deal with her disrespect. No good, that's what she is, just like her father and he was as bad as they come. Ask anybody, they'll tell you what he was like. . . .*

125

It was funny in a way. All this time Clare had been so worried about her face showing up on some milk carton. Why, she had even cut off all her hair—every inch of her only beauty—had made herself look like a regular freak, all on account of those stupid milk cartons. That was a laugh, wasn't it? Oh, that was a good one, all right. And yet—she knew it was crazy, but—she felt cheated somehow. It really *hurt* for some reason—that it had all been for nothing, that there had never even *been* any milk cartons. Not that she wanted to go back; of course she didn't—that had been the whole point, hadn't it? Of course it had. Still, there was this big stupid lump trying to form in her throat, so she choked it back, clenched her jaw. She had heard of crying over spilt milk but not over milk *cartons*.

The old man was still fumbling with words, trying to soft-pedal what Clare already knew: "But you see, Miss Caldwell, it's probably for the best right now, because the doctor doesn't think a long trip would be such a good idea— just yet anyway. He wants you to stay here in the hospital for a few more days, and then, why, then—if you would like, that is—" The old man paused there, as if he were embarrassed again, unsure how to put what he was trying to say. Suddenly he became preoccupied with the balloon strings, which he seemed surprised to find in his hand; he began tying them in an elaborate knot at the foot of the bed.

Griffey stepped into the gap: "And then you have a number of different options. That's where my agency comes in, you see. No need for anybody to live on the street, Clare, when there are so many people who want to help."

The County Dump for Troubled Teens, Clare could hear Thimble saying as Griffey continued: "I know of a couple of group homes that might have openings in a month or

126

two. I think you'd like that, living with others your own age."

Is that where your niece lives? Clare wanted to ask, but she held her tongue. Something told her this wasn't the time to be making accusations she only half understood; it wouldn't help matters to make *him* angry, too.

"And of course there's always the possibility of finding foster parents—if your mother doesn't feel differently later, after she's—had some time, you know. To think things over."

If she still says she doesn't want me back, you mean.

"And in the meantime," he went on, but now the old man—who had finally finished fiddling with the balloons—interrupted him.

"In the meantime your mother says you can stay with me," he blurted out, as if it had been stuck in his mouth, and he had only just now figured out how to rid himself of it.

Griffey nodded patiently. "Well, that is *one* possibility," he said. "But I'm not sure it's the best plan, after all. It's very generous of you, but we have to remember that you have a business to run, sir. And you're really under no obligation, you know. I'm afraid you're just overreacting to everything that's happened. It was only an accident, after all."

"If I hadn't left that door unlocked, she wouldn't be in this fix," A.J. repeated—more to his shoes, it seemed, than to anyone else in the room. But an obstinate line had appeared between the shaggy eyebrows; Clare could see it now as he looked up and added, "And her mother gave her permission, Mr. Griffey. You heard her. So it seems to me that it's up to Miss Caldwell."

Griffey smiled—that wonderfully warm reassuring sympathetic smile that had reminded her a little of Joey when she first saw him. *How could I ever have made a mistake like that?* she wondered. "Well, of course she did," he was saying. "She agreed to any arrangement we wanted to make, didn't she? But I'm not sure that Clare would be comfortable living over your—your place of business, or that *you* would be altogether comfortable either, playing nurse to a—what did your mother say, Clare? A not-quite-thirteen-year-old girl?" The smile deepened.

I'm going to throw up, she thought.

"No," he went on, "all and all, I think it would be better if Clare were with others her age, don't you? And I believe I know of a place where—"

"No!" Clare almost shouted it. Terror was rising in her again. She didn't know what Griffey had in mind; maybe it was perfectly all right. She had no proof otherwise, and it was possible that Cowboy had been mistaken about him. But then again, if he *wasn't* mistaken—her mind shied away from completing the thought; the possibility made her downright ill. She would stay with the old man until she was better; that was what she would do. She had thought she hated him, but that was a long time ago. He didn't seem all that terrible now—a little thick maybe, but that wasn't so bad; nothing could be so bad as having to go with the red-haired man. And anyhow it would only be for a little while, only until she was strong enough to run away again. And then she would find Cowboy and the others, and she would be no worse off than she had been before the tumble down the stairs, right? "No," she repeated, a little lower this time but even more firmly, if that were possible. "I'd rather stay with—with you," she said to the old man. Who blushed—actually *blushed*!—with pleasure.

"Well," he said, "that's fine, then. Just—just fine, Miss Caldwell." His mouth still didn't seem to know quite what to do with itself, but the mismatched eyes were smiling now.

The red-haired man sighed. "All right, then, Mr. Morgan. As you say, as long as you have the mother's permission, I guess it's really up to the two of you. But if it doesn't work out—"

"Excuse me?" Clare interrupted. For a second there—but she was hearing things, surely. Or maybe it was only one of those dumb coincidences. . . . Still—"Did you say," she began, but she couldn't bear to speak to the red-haired man, and so she turned to A.J. instead: "Did he call you Mr. Morgan?"

"Why, yes," he said. He seemed puzzled for some reason. "But I thought you knew. . . ."

"Knew what?" Clare asked, her voice suddenly small. She found she was holding her breath.

The old man just stood there for a little while, looking at her. After a moment he took his glasses out of his pocket—for no apparent reason, unless he needed them to *think* as well as to read—and put them on, balancing them carefully on their lone stem. And then he seemed to recollect himself somehow; he took them off again, shaking his head a little, as if at his own confusion. "I thought you knew," he repeated quietly, "that Joseph Morgan is my son."

16

THREE DAYS LATER the old man took her back to the hot-dog palace.

God must be up there laughing His head off, Clare thought. It was a good joke, wasn't it? Six weeks in the Twilight Zone, a cracked-up arm and a smashed-in head, just so she could end up right back where she had started? And Joey Morgan still just as far away as ever. Oh, it was rich, all right—a real knee-slapper. Probably had the whole angelic choir in stitches—

And that was even *before* they saw what she was wearing.

"Is there a—a bag I should send for?" the old man had asked the day before, when he stopped by the hospital to see how she was feeling.

Clare had felt herself coloring clear up to her caramel roots. "I don't need anything," she had said. "At home Ma—I mean, they used to say I never wore nothing but my cutoffs and the same old shirt."

"I see" was all he said at the time, but just before she left the hospital, the nurse had handed her a new pair of shorts and a white blouse with little yellow flowers on the collar.

"Where's my other stuff?" Clare asked, looking around for her standard Pink Floyd number.

"That was ruined," the nurse explained. "Bloodstains, you know."

"Oh," said Clare, pushing away the creepy image and pulling on the new clothes as quickly as she could, even if they did make her look like she had come straight from Bingo Night at St. Dork's.

And now, when the old man showed her to her room in the living quarters above the restaurant, she found three more pairs of shorts and five shirts and underwear and socks and a new toothbrush and toothpaste and even a little brassiere in a small pink box ("One Size Fits Most Beginners"— *good Lord!*)—all waiting for her, laid out neatly on the white comforter that covered the small iron bed. The closet door stood open, too; Clare could see several dresses hanging inside. *Dresses*, for crying out loud.

"I hope everything is all right," he said; the whole matter of clothing seemed to embarrass him to tears almost. "If anything doesn't—isn't right," he went on, waving vaguely in the direction of the pink box, then thinking better of it and putting his hand behind his back, as if it had shamed him somehow, "anything at all—why, you just let me know, won't you? And we'll—why, we'll just fix it."

What's his angle, anyhow? Clare wondered. *Ain't nobody that nice unless they're selling something.* But all she said was, "They look—fine. Just fine." And then she added, "Thanks"—pretty much directly to her shoes, which were a comfort to her, seeing as how they were still their own speedy-looking, ready-to-fly-away selves.

The old man smiled. "Well. That's good, then." He stood there smiling for a minute more—just stood there, as if he were waiting for some kind of cue. There was something else on his mind, that was pretty clear. *Joey Morgan?* Clare wondered. But she had no idea how to bring up the subject, so it just *hung* there between them like the Goodyear blimp, though for some reason they were both bound and determined to act as if they didn't notice it. And then finally after a while the old man said, "Well, I imagine you'll be wanting to rest now, won't you? So I'll just go along downstairs."

"Yes, sir," she said, since nothing else came to mind.

He stopped once more in the doorway, turned around. "Are you sure you're feeling all right, Miss Caldwell? The doctor said you could have another pain pill for your arm, if it bothers you."

She shook her head. "I'm okay," she said.

"All right, then. But Santiago and I will be just downstairs, if you need us," he said, and then he left her alone, closing the door quietly behind him.

This old guy's gonna bear watching, no question about it.

Clare put away her new dork clothes in the drawers of the small brown bureau next to the bed. Then she sat down on the little red rocking chair beside that—just sat there for a while, trying to get her brain in some kind of order. So much had happened so quickly; she was still trying to take it all in, to make herself believe where she was—

In Joey Morgan's room. The very same room he had had when he was a boy, the old man had told her—the room where he had grown up, had studied and slept and

132

dreamed a thousand dreams, practiced his magic tricks with coins and cards. Learned to play the saxophone, maybe.

And what a room it was! Like no other Clare had ever seen—a wonderful tower room, built in a perfect circle, with windows all around, windows covered in white muslin curtains, blowing softly, thrown open now to the sea breeze and the sounds and smells of the boardwalk. From here Clare could see everything—the whole island almost. The nice parts, anyhow: not the Baltic house and its rotting neighbors—those were hidden away to the west somewhere, behind the tall casino buildings—but the ocean and the sky to the east, the towering peaks of the Taj Mahal to the north, the tops of the green trees down south in Ventnor. Farther, even—almost all the way to Margate, where Racer claimed there was a giant elephant that had been in the movies. He had promised to show it to her someday. . . .

The thought made her throat ache. *Where is he now?* she wondered. She leaned out the window, strained her eyes up and down the length of the boardwalk, trying to catch a glimpse of the gang. She still hadn't seen them since that last disastrous night, and she was worried about them. Though of course there was probably no way they could have chanced a visit to the hospital, with all those official-looking people around—if they even knew she was *in* the hospital, that is, if they hadn't finally given up on her altogether.

But there was no sign of them, only the usual crowd: an old lady stopping to help her slow-moving husband— "How you doing, Roy?" Clare could hear her asking as she straightened his baseball cap; a small shining-faced boy who was charging up the stairs from the beach with a Styrofoam cup in his hands—"Look what *I* got!" he exclaimed, showing its contents to a smiling bearded man. And the crippled woman, lying on her cot in front of Caesar's, playing her keyboard:

Sometimes I'm happy,
Sometimes I'm blue. . . .

What does it mean, anyway, Clare wondered, *to be happy?* She had never really given it much thought before. Had Joey Morgan been happy in this room? And if he had, then why had he gone away? Why had he stayed away such a long time? As far as she could remember, in nearly five years he had never once mentioned a father in Atlantic City. "Back east," he would say, when anyone asked where he came from; nothing more. What could have happened here to make him so silent?

Clare began to look around the room, searching for clues. It was all still pretty much as he had left it, she guessed, except for the new girl's things in the drawers and closet and the fluffy coverlet on the bed—bought just for her, she suspected, judging from the crisp whiteness of it and the department-store smell still hanging around its edges.

Otherwise this was definitely a boy's room. An old Phillies pennant was tacked up over the headboard, next to a framed photograph of a pitcher named Robin Roberts, which was hanging right beside an even larger photo—this one autographed—of Stan Getz playing his saxophone. And then there was a whole bookcase filled with assorted mementos: old sports trophies, Hardy Boys books, a purple dog— or was it a turtle?—made out of papier-mâché in some long-ago art class. Models, too—a shelf full of them—cars and boats and planes like the ones hanging in the restaurant downstairs. And several pictures of a skinny kid with big ears—*Joey?* One of him in a Little League uniform, another of him holding his sax. Still another of the same boy, a bit older now maybe, seated beside a pretty dark-haired woman in an old-timey biplane. They were laughing, sharing some secret joke, it appeared, while just in front of them in the cockpit a younger version of the old man smiled proudly at the camera. "First Flight of *Morgan's Folly*" said the caption on the bottom. "Atlantic City, New Jersey, May 29, 1965."

Something stirred in Clare's memory, turned over in her stomach. Just a crazy image—nothing most likely; she had just fallen on her head, after all. And yet—she could almost have sworn . . .

She crossed the room, opened the door, stepped out into the hall. Then she climbed carefully down the winding metal staircase that led to the dining room.

Santiago saw her first. The sharp dark eyes glanced up from behind the soda wheel and immediately registered suspicion. *He don't trust me,* Clare thought, *but then why should he?* He had probably put two and two together by now, unlike his boss, who for some reason had never noticed—or at least never brought it up if he *had* noticed—Clare's part in the peculiar goings-on the night of the storm.

But all Santiago said now was, "Are you hurting, miss? A.J. said maybe you would need one of your pills."

"No, thank you," said Clare. Actually her arm *was* beginning to ache again, but the pills made her groggy, and she wanted her mind to be perfectly clear. "I just need to ask Mr. Morgan a question."

"Something I could tell you, maybe? He's busy right now—just gone down to his workshop."

"This will only take a minute," she said, starting in that direction.

But Santiago hurried out from behind the counter. "No, miss—he don't allow no one down there. You wait here, please. I will call him for you."

Santiago hustled past her to the No Admittance door, tried the knob. It was locked. "I forget," he muttered. "A.J.—he's more careful since—he's more careful now." He began to knock briskly, at the same time pushing a button for what looked to be a newly installed buzzer.

A minute later Clare heard footsteps coming up the cellar stairs, and then the door opened, and A.J. was standing there, concern already breaking out in deep furrows on his forehead. "Are you ill, Miss Caldwell?" he asked.

"No, sir," she answered. "It's just—well, I guess this sounds crazy, but—" She broke off, glanced at Santiago, then down at her feet. She hated sounding like such a nut case in front of him; he thought little enough of her as it was.

A.J. seemed to understand. "It's all right, Santiago," he said. "Thank you for calling me."

"No sweat, A.J.," he said, and then he turned away—reluctantly, it seemed to Clare—and went back to the counter.

"Now," said A.J., "what is it, Miss Caldwell?" He lowered his voice even more. "If there's something wrong about"—he was blushing again—"about the clothes, why, we can change them."

"No, it's not that. It's just—"

"What is it, miss? Please—if there's anything troubling you—anything at all—you'll tell me, won't you?"

"Yes, sir." Clare took a deep breath. "I was just wondering—is there an airplane in your basement?"

Now it was A.J.'s turn to fall silent. He looked at Clare for a moment, then over at Santiago, who was busy with a customer now, then back at Clare. The color in his cheeks had deepened to a brilliant scarlet. He cleared his throat, smiled a little. "Does it matter?" he asked.

"Yes," said Clare, feeling strangely excited. "It does."

"Well, then," said the old man, moving aside and holding the door open for Clare to walk through, "watch your step, Miss Caldwell."

17

SLOWLY, CAREFULLY, Clare descended the basement stairs, holding tightly to the wooden railing. She had to steel herself against the memory of the last time she had come this way—well, not *this* way, exactly, since now she was on her feet. Even so, the terror of that night was still a sickening weight in the pit of her stomach. But she had to see again with her own eyes, really see this time—

That she hadn't been dreaming, after all.

It was standing in the center of the cavernous room, beneath the frosted windows—not another miniature but a full-size plane, the old-timey sort with double wings and an open cockpit. Silver colored, it was, except for the deep burnished wood of its propeller and the glossy black of the bird in flight that was painted on its side, just above the words *Morgan's Folly*.

The plane in the picture, thought Clare. *No way . . .*

Even now, with a whole row of strong lights shining down on it from overhead, there was still something unreal about it; something so downright peculiar that you would never expect to find it anywhere but in a dream—one of those wild visions that come from eating pizza with extra cheese and onions directly before going to bed. Certainly not in somebody's basement—

"It's an aeroplane," the old man said quietly, running a prideful finger along the tip of a silver wing. "An a-e-r-o-p-l-a-n-e—that's the way they spelled it in the old days."

"But—" Clare stammered, "but what's it doing down here?"

The old man smiled shyly. "I built it," he said.

Clare's jaw dropped. "You *built* it? You built a whole air—I mean, aeroplane? All by *yourself*?"

"Oh, no," he said. "Not all by myself. I had a lot of help through the years. . . ." His voice trailed off.

Here comes that blimp again, thought Clare. *Well, go on, girl. You got questions, spit 'em out. It's what you came down here for, ain't it?* She looked him in the eye. "Did Joey—Joseph—help?" she asked.

The old man seemed almost grateful to have the name out in the open. "Oh, my, yes," he said. "I couldn't have done it without him." A.J. took a handkerchief out of his back pocket, started wiping a spot on the immaculate propeller—some infinitesimal smudge visible only to him. "Of course he was just a little fellow when we started—scarcely five years old. All we had at first was an engine and a set of blueprints—just the *idea* of a plane, really. But Joseph—he could see it even then. 'When's it gonna fly, Pop?' he used to ask me. 'When's it gonna fly?'" The old man shook his head, chuckled a little. He stopped polishing now, looked down at the handkerchief for a while, as if it might hold some sort of message; the clue to a puzzle maybe.

He misses him, too, thought Clare. And then she steeled herself against the stupid mushy feeling that brought on: *Well, so what if he does? It's his own fault probably. No way Joey would have left if there hadn't been a good reason.* But she couldn't very well just ask him outright, not about *that*; no way he would have told her the truth anyhow. Instead she asked:

"So how long did he have to wait? Until it flew, I mean?"

The old man looked surprised by her question—almost as if he had forgotten she was still in the room. "Oh, well," he said, "we made so many mistakes. It took us quite a while." His smile was apologetic. "About ten years, off and on."

Ten years! So Joey was fifteen in that picture upstairs, when everybody still looked so happy? "That's a long time," said Clare. She was thinking of the only thing she and Mama had ever tried to build together—a jigsaw puzzle picture of the Eiffel Tower that some relative had given them for Christmas one year. Jessie had gotten sick of it after the first forty-five minutes—all those frustrating little pieces of blue sky. "Let's just frame the cover," she had said. "It's prettier when it ain't all cut up anyhow. . . ."

The old man looked thoughtful. "It's funny," he said. "It doesn't seem so long to me now." He turned to the plane again, began to move the handkerchief lightly over its silver side, toward the double set of passenger seats behind the cockpit. "At first we thought about building something a little smaller, to save time. But Joseph wanted there to be room enough for a whole family." A.J. chuckled quietly. "He had this idea we could give up the restaurant business, make our living like the old barnstormers, you know? Flying from one town to the next, taking customers for a spin in the air. Sounded pretty good, to tell the truth."

Well, sure, Clare thought. *It all* sounds *good—like raspberry jam on toast. So where's the seeds, buster? What is it you ain't telling me?* "You fly it much now?" she asked casually.

"No," said the old man. He looked embarrassed again for some reason. "Not so much anymore. It's been—a while."

"Why?" Clare asked. "Is it broken?"

"Oh, no, no, it's not broken. I've just been making a few—adjustments lately. Upkeep, really, nothing major. Just to be sure it's ready."

"Ready for what?"

The old man didn't answer right away. He went to work with his handkerchief again, this time cleaning the lenses of his one-stemmed glasses. "Miss Caldwell," he began, then stopped, cleared his throat. *Blimp time,* thought Clare.

"Yes, sir?" she asked, trying to keep the impatience out of her voice.

"I've been meaning to tell you," he said to the glasses, "that we might have an address for Joseph now."

Clare's heart did a cartwheel in her chest. "He wrote you? Joey wrote?"

The old man shook his head. "Well, no—not *directly*. It was more of a—a business matter, you see. . . ." He hesitated, then went on haltingly when Clare still looked blank. "There was a note we signed jointly—for a car he bought when he was here last fall."

Bill collectors, thought Clare. *Who'da ever believed I'd be thanking those guys for anything?* She almost laughed out loud. "So this address they gave you—do you think it's good? Have you written him? Did you try calling information?" She couldn't get the questions out fast enough now.

"There's no number listed," said the old man. "But I wrote several weeks ago, and my letter wasn't returned, so I'm assuming the address is all right. I could—well, I could give it to you, if you'd like."

If she'd *like*! Was he kidding? "Well, sure, that'd be great! That'd be—" She broke off, suddenly wary, even in the middle of her excitement. The old man had planned this, hadn't he? He *wanted* her to write Joey; he was using her as—as bait, that's what, thinking that maybe even if his son didn't want to see him anymore, he might come for Clare. Was *that* his angle? *Well, shoot,* she thought, *what if it is? What does it matter, as long as I get Joey Morgan?* Still, when she spoke again, it was more quietly, so as to cover the pounding of her heart. "That'd be—okay, I guess."

The old man smiled a small, pleased smile. "Fine," he said. "I'll just—well, I'll just get that for you right away." He crossed the room to a large worktable that was littered with tools and odd-looking pieces of machinery and magazines and newspapers and mail, came back with a small slip of paper with Joey's name and new West Hollywood, California, address written out in small, precise cursive.

"Thanks," she said, trying to keep her voice even, her burning face averted. It wouldn't do to let the old man see her trembling, would it?

She was halfway up the stairs when a crazy thought

made her turn around, go back. There was no way, was there? "Uh, Mr. Morgan?"

"Yes, miss?"

"I was just thinking, the stairs are so narrow, you couldn't—I mean, that plane is so *big*. How'd you ever get it out of here?"

The old man's smile widened. "Just watch," he said. And then he walked over to a set of switches on the far wall, flipped one. And all at once there was a terrific humming, grinding noise, and the whole wall seemed to come to life, and then Clare saw that it *wasn't* a wall, really; it was an enormous door—the kind that people have on their garages, only much bigger. And now it was opening onto the vacant lot next door, and the basement was flooded with sunlight, and there was that crazy plane sparkling in it, its silver nose pointing to the blue-skied horizon, while up above on the boardwalk people stopped and stared.

"Look, Daddy!" cried a little boy. "It's a airplane!"

You gotta be kidding me, thought Clare. She turned in amazement to the old man, who was standing there quietly, watching her with that small, pleased expression on his face again—half-proud, half-shy. "How in the heck . . . ?" she began.

"It was Joseph's idea," he said.

"Oh," Clare murmured, walking over to the magic wall. She was wondering just what Joey had had in mind—a quick getaway, it looked like. She pictured him with his sleeves rolled up, hacking away, hammering and chiseling, chain-sawing his way out of—out of *what?* Not just this old basement, surely. "Yeah," she said, "he used to fix a lot of stuff around the apartment."

The old man looked as if she had just given him a present. "Oh, did he? Well, that's—that's nice to hear. . . . He used to fix things, did he? Oh, yes, he was always good with his hands." He lowered his eyes, studied his own hands, as if looking for some resemblance. And it struck Clare again, how much he missed his son—whether he deserved to or not—how anxious he was for any little scrap of news about him. *Just like me*, she thought.

And then it occurred to her: they each had pieces of him, didn't they? Her Joey, his Joseph. And maybe if they put them together, they would almost add up to a whole person. . . .

Aw, gimme a break, she told herself. *Just hang on to your own pieces, sister. They're slippery enough as it is.*

And with that in mind she tucked away the new address in her pocket and hurried back up the stairs.

18

Dear Joey, she began, *how are you, fine I hope. Well, it's been a long time since—* But that sounded incredibly stupid, so she wadded up that version and sent it flying to take its place alongside its seventeen brothers and sisters in the wastebasket.

Dear Joey, she tried again, *well maybe you won't beleave this but here I am in your old room in Atlantic City—* She crumpled that one, too; maybe he wouldn't want to be reminded of his old room.

Dear Joey— She stopped there, sat chewing on her pen. How could she put it into words—all the things that had happened? The longer she tried, the harder it got. The thought of those other letters—the ones she had thrown into the ocean—still made her cringe; she wasn't about to beg like *that* again. No telling where this one was going to end up; she didn't want some nosy bill collector giggling over her personal life, for crying out loud. Still, if there was even a *chance* that Joey would really get it . . .

Dear Joey, she wrote at last, after agonizing for another half an hour, *I left Nashville because it was bad there with you gone so I came here to your dads looking for you but you were all ready in California. So anyhow I was wondering, could I come live with you now? I really need to Joey I can't go back there, I wouldn't ask you if it wasn't important. Love, Clare.*

She put down her pen, read it over. Well, it wasn't near good enough, but it was the best she could do. And if it ever made it to Joey—well, he would just have to understand, that was all.

She turned out the light, lay back on the little white bed. *Must be after midnight now*, she thought, watching the moonlight slipping around the edges of the softly moving curtains. *Where are Cowboy and the others tonight?*

With the thought came a tug of guilt. For hours now her mind had been so full of Joey Morgan that there had been no room for anything else. How could she have forgotten them, even for a little while? Here she was lying with a full belly in a clean, soft bed in her own room—much nicer than any motel, even—while they were—who knew where? Back with the rats maybe, or on Baltic still, worrying about her. Or *weren't* they worrying about her? Either possibility was bad, the second even worse than the first. She would have to find them tomorrow, that was all there was to it; there was so much she had to tell them. She had dreaded it before—having to admit what a klutz she had been, what a mess she had made of things. But now—why, maybe it had turned out there really *was* a kind of treasure in the old man's basement. Better than Boardwalk—oh, yes, better than anything. If her crazy tumble down the cellar stairs

146

wound up taking her clear to California, it would be a kind of miracle, wouldn't it? *Almost enough to make a person start believing in God again*, she thought, as her eyes closed and she began to drift off. . . .

A miracle for you, you mean. Don't do much for the rest of us, does it? It was almost as if Thimble were standing right outside the window, so clearly could Clare hear her say the words. She *was* there, wasn't she? Tapping on the pane—*tap, tap, tapping* like the spooky blackbird in the poem that nut Mrs. Byars had read aloud in English class last year—with the last word in bird-talk, no less, so she sounded like a crazed parakeet: "Quoth the Raven, 'Nevermore.' " . . . *Go away, bird, go away, Thimble. The pain pills are making me goofy.* . . .

But there it came again: *tap, tap, tapping*—louder this time, real enough to make her sit up straight, then climb out of bed, go to the window, lift the white curtain just as another shower—of *what*? Pebbles? Broken-up seashells?— came spattering against the pane. She looked down on the boardwalk now and saw not just Thimble but five familiar faces looking back at her. All five of them: Cowboy, too, and Little Dog and Racer and even Shoe, who was grinning his widest and wearing a pair of blue sunglasses. *Mine?* Clare wondered. Racer must have read her mind; he pointed at them and waved gleefully.

Good Lord, she thought, *they're out of their minds!* And yet at the same time a wave of love washed over her: they must have been watching her from a distance all this time, then, keeping an eye on her. They hadn't abandoned her; they had just been waiting for the right moment—

Come down, Cowboy motioned to her, pointing toward the front door.

No, she tried to tell him, shaking her head. *This ain't the right moment. The old man might still be awake. I'm all right; I'll find you tomorrow.*

But Cowboy only looked impatient. *Come on!* he waved again. *Before somebody sees us!*

Clare sighed. She would have to go down; they would never understand otherwise. *All right, I'm coming!* she nodded. And then as quickly and noiselessly as she could manage with the stupid cast in her way, she put on a shirt and a pair of the dork shorts, slipped into her sneakers, and tiptoed out into the hall. She waited at the top of the spiral staircase, listened for any sound that would tell her the old man was still about, heard nothing. Then she made her way silently down the stairs, across the restaurant, unlocked the front door—there was only an old-fashioned latch, after all—

And then she was outside; she was on the boardwalk, and the gang was all over her: Shoe handing her the shades, barely managing to hold in his giggles; Racer pounding her on the back and whispering, "Old Hatso, hey, man, what do you say? Thought you was never gonna see our ugly mugs again, did you?"; Little Dog solemnly shaking her good hand; Cowboy, holding back a little, watching, but he was smiling, too; and even Thimble might have looked a shade less menacing than usual.

"Come on, you guys," Cowboy said after a minute, "let's move out before somebody comes." He looked at Clare, put a gentle hand on her good shoulder. "Can you make it all right?" he asked.

"Sure," she said, trying to sound casual, when in fact his touch had sent a zillion kilowatts of electricity charging through her.

"Good man," he said. "Just over to the parking garage. The other places are too far for now."

"All right," she said, and almost added, *but I can't stay*, then thought better of it. *No*, she told herself, *not yet. How am I going to explain it to him?*

They were there in no time at all, climbing in through the broken slat. Clare shrank back instinctively from the gaping black maw before her, then forced herself to go on. Amazing how quickly she had grown unused to it. But once they were all safely inside, Little Dog turned on one of the flashlights; that helped a little. They gathered around it like a tribe of primitive cavemen before their sacred fire.

Everyone looked at Cowboy, waited for him to begin. "Okay," he said, turning the brown eyes on Clare, "first business on the agenda—" Suddenly he smiled. "Welcome back, Hat. You had us pretty worried for a while there."

It nearly brought tears to her eyes. How could she ever tell him she wasn't going to stay? She had loused up everything, fallen on her head, even, and she was still *in*? It didn't make sense, surely; by all rights she should have failed the test. But he had called her Hat. . . .

"Thanks," she muttered, and then they were all shaking her hand and patting her gingerly on the back: "Yeah, man, way to go." "Glad to see you, Hat." "Shoot, we didn't know *what* to think."

Thimble was still holding back a little. "What happened that night, anyhow?"

"Yeah," Racer added, "what was the deal? We bribed one of them beach kids to check it out the next morning, but they wouldn't tell him nothing 'cept you was in the hospital. What was it, man? They beat you up or what?"

Clare shook her head. "No, it wasn't like that." And

then she told the story—all of it, as well as she could remember, leaving out only the part about the red-haired man, since she wasn't sure if Cowboy would want her to mention him in front of the others. But everything else, all the way from her accident on the stairs clear through to her second trip to the basement this afternoon. And when she got to the crazy silver plane that the old man had built down there, Racer's mouth dropped open.

"A *real* plane, Hatso? You sure it ain't just another one of them models he gots hanging all over the place?"

"No," said Clare. "It's the real thing. He knows how to fly it and everything—I saw a picture."

"Aw, man, that's the coolest thing I ever heard! We gotta see that, don't we, Shoe?"

Shoe's eyes were shining. He made a plane with his hands, flew it up over his head.

"Forget it," said Thimble. "Who cares about some homemade hunk of junk in a basement? You want to see a real plane, go over to Bader Field, that's all."

"No," said Little Dog; he was bright-eyed, too. "It's different when you build something from scratch. Me and my dad—" And then he broke off suddenly, remembering himself. "I mean, well, I wouldn't mind seeing that plane, that's all. . . ."

Only Cowboy seemed not to care one way or another about the plane. He was looking at Clare. "This guy—the old man's son—he's a friend of yours? A sort of—relative, you said?"

Clare had touched only lightly on that part of her story, hoping to break it to the others in little pieces maybe, that wouldn't be so hard to swallow. "Sort of," she murmured.

"And now you want to hang around there, is that it? To wait for him? To see if he calls or something?"

"What?" Racer jumped in when Clare hesitated. "Hatso don't want to live with the hot-dog man! She's *in* now, she's with us—ain't that right, Hatso?"

They were all looking at her now. "Well, sure," she began. "I mean, I *want* to stay with y'all, but—"

"But you don't need us anymore." Thimble's left eyebrow shot up. "That's it, ain't it, kid? You got other friends now."

"No," Clare said. "I mean—y'all are still my friends. It's just—Joey—"

Cowboy held up a hand. "It's okay, Hat. You don't have to explain if you don't want to. But this guy—are you sure he's all right? You can trust him?"

Clare nodded. "If you knew him, you'd see."

Cowboy thought this over for a moment, then continued. "And the old man—what about him? I don't want you going back there if he's—you know, weird or anything."

Weird? Was that the word for A.J.? Clare could still see him: how miserable he had looked, trying to tie those dumb balloons to her hospital bed; the way he had blushed over the pink box in the tower room; his small, pleased smile when he showed her the magic wall. . . . Oh, sure, he was weird, all right, but not the way Cowboy meant. "No," she said, "I can handle him."

Thimble sniffed. "He the one bought you those clothes?"

Now Clare's face was burning. She shrugged. "He's just old, is all."

"Don't mean nothing." Racer was shaking his head.

"Old ones is the worst sometimes. Don't trust him, Hatso. Stick with us."

"Who cares?" Thimble asked. "You want out—well, who's stopping you? You think *we* need you?"

This stung. Clare lifted her chin. "It ain't like that," she said. "I mean—I'd still be with the gang. I could do us more good from the inside, maybe."

"What's that supposed to mean?" Thimble wanted to know. "Inside what?"

"Inside the old man's place," Clare explained, scrambling to put her thoughts into words as soon as they tumbled into her head. "I mean, it's a hot-dog joint, right? All the food we want—for free, don't you get it? Wouldn't be nothing to it—I just wait until the old man goes to bed at night, same as now, see? And then I take whatever we need and beat it out here. Easy as pie."

Little Dog's ears were twitching. "Free food?" He looked at Cowboy. "Might not be a bad idea."

"It don't work like that," said Thimble, shaking her head. "You're with us or you ain't, that's all. Can't have it both ways, right, Cowboy?"

Cowboy didn't answer right away. He stood up, started pacing back and forth before the little circle.

"I don't know, Hatso." Racer looked doubtful. "But maybe—this way—you think you could get us in to see that plane?"

"Sure," said Clare, putting on her best confident act. "No sweat."

"Hear that, Shoe?" Racer beamed at his friend. "Gonna take us a ride maybe!"

Shoe grinned, glided his pretend plane in a graceful loop.

But Thimble was frowning. "What's the deal, Cowboy? The new girl can't be in and out at the same time, can she? We ain't never done it like that before."

Cowboy stopped pacing. He looked only at Clare. "It means that much to you, Hat? This guy—your friend—he means that much?"

Everyone was quiet, waiting for her to speak. It was her decision, then; Cowboy was leaving it up to her. So why did she suddenly feel as if she were tied to a herd of wild horses going eight different directions at once? Still, she took a deep breath, made herself meet Cowboy's eyes. "I gotta know, that's all," she said.

19

CLARE PULLED DOWN the metal handle of the mailbox, dropped her letter inside. "Okay, Joey," she whispered, as the door slammed shut with a hollow *clang!* "Your move."

And then the waiting began.

Sometimes it seemed as if all she *did* that August was wait—wait for the mail to come, wait for the phone to ring, wait every night while the old man closed up the restaurant and got ready for bed. This took an eternity. First he would fiddle around forever in the basement, fooling with that crazy old plane. Then he would plod back up to the kitchen and rattle every pan in the place, it sounded like, stirring up one little pot of hot chocolate, which he would carry up with two mugs on a tray to the small upstairs den, where Clare would be sitting, staring at the television, trying to hide her impatience.

"Do you mind if I join you, Miss Caldwell?" he would

ask every time, setting his tray on the old trunk that served as a coffee table.

And of course she would say, "No, sir. Thank you, sir," because what else could she do? And then they would sit there for another century or so, sipping their cocoa, with David Letterman or whoever doing all the talking for them, until at last the old man's gray head would begin nodding, and Clare would say, "Well, I guess I'll turn in now, Mr. Morgan."

And he would start awake and stand up and say, "Oh, yes. My goodness, it's late, isn't it? Good-night, Miss Cald-well. I hope you rest well."

Clare would say thanks then and pretend to go off to bed in the tower room, but all the time she was just waiting for the line of yellow light at the bottom of her door to disappear, signaling that the old man had finally turned off the lamp in his room.

She would force herself to wait awhile more after that, just to make sure he was really asleep, and then she would tiptoe down to the kitchen and gather her supplies in a large shopping bag—choosing carefully so as not to be easily detected: the buns at the back of the big bread bin, the leftover fries, a king-size package of hot dogs from the bottom of the stack in the refrigerator, a carton of chili, an old gallon milk jug, rinsed out and filled with soda from the wheel. And then she would slip out silently into the night. . . .

"Aw, man, this is great!" said Racer, plowing his way through his third dog and second bowl of chili in one sitting. Hot, even; Cowboy had lifted a miniature camper's stove and several cylinders of propane from the sporting-goods department at O'Farrell's and set it up in the depths of the old garage. "You sure they ain't missing all this stuff?"

Clare shook her head. "The old man wouldn't notice if his own nose caught fire," she said.

"I'm sick of hot dogs," grumped Thimble, flinging away half of hers. "Anyway, how do we know he ain't on to you? He could poison us all, and we wouldn't have a clue till it was too late."

"How could he do that without poisoning his customers, too?" Cowboy asked.

"I don't know," Thimble admitted grudgingly. "I don't like it, that's all."

"Shoot," Clare muttered to Racer. "She ain't never liked anything before; why start now?"

But nobody else seemed to have any objections. The guys packed away food enough for a small army, except for Shoe maybe, and he had never been all that big an eater. He reminded Clare of the odd little plant that sat on the kitchen table back home—the only bit of green in the apartment that Jessie had never managed to kill, simply because it didn't need anything, not water or plant food or even sunlight. "It eats air," she had explained happily. Which Clare sometimes thought must be what accounted for Shoe's survival, too.

Little Dog, now, he was in hog heaven—and not just because he *was* a big eater. "Don't knock it," he told Thimble, while he scribbled contentedly in his notebook with one hand and licked hot-dog grease off the fingers of the other. "Free food is free food."

It was a good thing, too, because their usual resources had dried up just lately, due to the fact that the cops had

156

suddenly decided to wage an all-out war against petty theft on the boardwalk.

"Aw, man, they're *everywhere*," Racer told Clare disgustedly. "It's getting so you can't even hawk a lucky number without somebody looking at you crooked."

"It's just the politicians," Little Dog explained. "Happens every time there's an election. Some guy starts spouting off in the papers about how Atlantic City's going to the dogs, and then the mayor gets to worrying about his job, and next thing you know you got cops on every corner. One of 'em almost grabbed Racer and Shoe today, did you hear?"

"*What?*"

"Aw, it wasn't no big deal," said Racer, his mouth full of french fries. "We was trying to do a little ketchup business, that's all. How was we supposed to know that old dude was one of the blue boys? Ain't no fair when they don't wear their suits."

"You tried to rob a policeman?" Clare was aghast. "How'd you get away?"

Racer shrugged. "Shoot, man, wasn't nothing we couldn't *handle*. I mean, we woulda outran him easy anyway."

Thimble rolled her eyes. "Don't believe a word. They'da both been dead ducks if Cowboy hadn't been watching."

"I ain't saying we weren't glad to see him," Racer said with dignity.

Thimble laughed out loud at that. "I guess you were." She looked at Clare. "Cop has 'em both by the scruff of the neck when Cowboy sees 'em. He can spot one of those guys a mile away. 'Yell,' he tells me, and then he acts like he's stealing *my* money, get it? And I'm standing there yelling and pointing, while he takes off down the boardwalk. So the cop drops these two and goes after him. Can't come near him, acourse. Cowboy's ten times faster 'n any blue boy. And naturally by the time the cop comes back to see about me, I'm long gone, too—me and both these bozos."

Racer looked injured. "Oughta been wearing his suit, that's all."

Cowboy shook his head. "You know better than that, Racer. You can't trust those guys. They aren't ever gonna do what you want 'em to. You have to think quicker than they do. That's your only chance. All it takes is one slipup and you're gone, man."

"Aw, Cowboy, you know we woulda outran him."

"I know you were lucky today. You guys just cool it for a while, you hear? Heat won't be on forever. Mayor'll get reelected or else he won't; either way the cops'll get tired of missing their favorite soap operas and things'll go back to normal. In the meantime we lie low, that's all. Nobody's gonna starve, right, Hat?"

Clare blushed at the compliment, but the truth was the responsibility made her doubly nervous. She was taking a little more each night from the hot-dog palace—not just the restaurant fare but bits and pieces of the old man's personal supply, too: a box of cereal, a carton of milk, a few oranges and carrots here and there. All of which was maybe more likely to be missed, but what could she do? Thimble was right; you couldn't live on hot dogs forever. What was it those old-time sailors used to get before they figured out about vitamins? Scurvy or rickets or some such disgusting disease; Clare could still hear her old science teacher's horror stories about black teeth and shriveled eyeballs or whatever. She didn't believe she could have stood it if even one of Cowboy's pretty teeth had fallen out.

Anyhow, so far the old man hadn't said a word about the missing food, just kept smiling his shy smile and treating her with that careful courtesy that made her feel as if they were both characters in one of those old black-and-white movies made in England or some weird place like that: "Good morning, Miss Caldwell," he would say when Clare joined him for breakfast—or lunch, really; after her late nights with the gang she hardly ever managed to drag her aching arm and her throbbing head out of bed before noon. "Did you sleep well? Awfully humid again today, I'm afraid. I hope you won't be too uncomfortable in that cast. . . ." And Clare would nod politely and murmur her "Yes, sirs" and "No, sirs," but all the time she was still trying to figure out if he was just plain dense or the biggest fraud since all-night cough syrup.

Santiago was another story. Clare avoided his sharp eyes whenever she could, but she could feel them on her all the same, watching her every move. And finally one day about three weeks into the boardwalk crackdown, he was waiting for her when she came down the spiral staircase.

"Excuse me, miss."

His tone made her stomach tighten. "What is it?" she said, trying to sound casual. She would have turned and fled back upstairs if she had thought it would do any good, but that would have been a flat admission of guilt, wouldn't it? She glanced around the room; the old man was nowhere in sight. *Okay, girl, you got to tough it out, that's all. Ain't nothing he can prove—*

"Miss . . ." Santiago lowered his voice. "I don't like to make trouble for you. You're a—friend of the family, I guess. But A.J., he's like a big kid sometime, trusting every-body. I say to him, 'Listen, A.J., there are some who can't deserve to be trusted. This is the boardwalk, man.' But he's living in his own world still, not thinking of nothing but his boy and that crazy plane."

Clare lifted her chin. "And you don't think he should trust *me*, is that what you're saying?"

Santiago scowled, folded his arms. "Here's what I'm saying, miss. Maybe A.J. don't want to remember nothing wrong about that night when you—hurt yourself. Maybe he don't keep track so good when food he pays plenty for ain't there no more where it's supposed to be. But I'm knowing what I know. You and your—friends, whoever they are—you should watch yourselves. A.J.—he's *my* friend. First one I ever make when I come into this country, best one, too. Anybody wants to be messing with him, they got to step past Santiago first."

Clare's chin went higher still. "Is that all?"

"That's all," he said, nodding darkly. He walked back to the kitchen then and started grilling a cheese sandwich for her lunch—which she ate in silence, doing her best to look as if his words meant nothing to her, though this wasn't easy with her face afire and her mind racing: what, exactly, did his veiled threats mean?

Santiago knew about the food—if she kept taking it, would he call the police? But she couldn't stop now, could she? Not when the gang was depending on her more than ever. Only last night she had learned that there had been more trouble—

"Saw a friend of yours today, Hatso," Racer had told her. "Didn't we, Shoe?"

160

Shoe acted as if he hadn't heard the question. His giggle motor was silent for a change; he was lying listlessly on the concrete block, his head in Thimble's lap.

"What friend?" Clare asked.

"Old Ginger—the waitress down at the Rexall, remember her? The one chased us that day you walked the check."

Clare remembered, all right. She was glad it was too dark for anybody to see her coloring up again. "Sure," she said. "How is old Ginger, anyway?"

Racer chuckled. "Still in a bad mood." He shook his head in fake wonderment. "Can't understand it—I don't think she likes me!"

Cowboy didn't laugh. "It's not funny, Racer. You should've told us she had it in for you. You came half an inch from getting caught, don't you know that?"

"Shoot." Racer was unperturbed. He took his old pirate eye patch out of his pocket, began twirling it on the end of his finger. "I been knowing Ginger from way back. She ain't gonna mess with me over one little bottle of pink medicine."

"Medicine?" Clare asked. "Is somebody—" Her eyes went to Shoe's limp figure. "Is he sick?"

Racer bent over his friend, pushed a sweaty-looking strand of hair off his forehead. "Naw," he said, "old Shoe ain't sick, are you, bro? He just got the stomachache, that's all. He's okay now. Pink medicine plugged him right up, didn't it?"

"Too many hot dogs, that's what got him," Thimble muttered, stroking his cheek.

Clare ignored her insult, but she made a mental note to see if she could find something more soothing for Shoe's next supper—soup maybe, that was what Mama would have said, wasn't it? Clare was pretty sure she remembered seeing a can or two in the back of the old man's cupboard. . . .

She thought of it again as she sat worrying over her grilled cheese. It didn't matter what Santiago said. She couldn't chicken out on her friends, not now.

That night it seemed to her that the old man had never taken so long going to bed.

"What's this you're watching, Miss Caldwell? A nature show?" he asked, setting his tray on the old trunk. "Well, I'll just join you, if you don't mind. These are always so interesting, aren't they?"

"Yes, sir," Clare murmured, though she hadn't been paying full attention to the television, just staring at the screen and listening to the fitful clatter of her own brain, while the narrator went on about the war between lions and hyenas over in Africa.

"Oh, my. Oh, the poor thing," the old man said, shaking his head over a sick lioness that was stumbling blindly toward some river's edge. "What's wrong with her, do you know?"

"Hmm? Oh." Clare roused herself with an effort. "She's snake-bit," she explained. "She went off by herself to have her babies, only a cobra got her. Got the kids, too—they're dead already. But she's bigger, see—stronger. So the poison takes longer with her."

"Oh, my," the old man said again. He was leaning forward now; the deep creases had appeared once more between his eyebrows.

For crying out loud, she felt like telling him, *it's only a TV show*. But his concern was contagious somehow; she sat up a little straighter herself, watched with him as the lioness quenched her raging thirst and then collapsed a little way from the water, waiting to die.

Yip yap yowlll! came a bloodcurdling sound from the surrounding darkness.

"What's that?" the old man asked.

"It's the hyenas," Clare explained patiently—though the narrator was doing a fine job, if A.J. would only listen. "They'll get her now she's so weak, see? Wouldn'ta had a chance if she was healthy and with her friends, but they know she's in trouble tonight."

"I see," said the old man. He and Clare were both quiet for a while then, watching, while the hyenas moved their hideous faces closer to their prey. They were circling now, snarling shadows flickering in the moonlight, howling their unearthly laughter. *Worse than wolves,* Clare thought, *that noise they make. Yip yap yowllling, coming closer and closer . . .*

"Good Lord," said the old man, "this is terrible."

The hyenas were on her now, and the lioness was trying to fight them. She was blind from the poison, bleeding, but still she fought back; she roared and struck out with her claws at her unseen enemies. *But she don't have a chance, does she?* Clare thought. *Ain't no way she can win—*

Suddenly Clare felt sick. She couldn't watch any more of this. She stood up. "I guess—I guess I'll go on to bed now," she said.

The old man stood up, too. "They shouldn't show such things," he murmured, flicking off the television.

"Probably all fake anyhow," said Clare.

"Maybe so," he said. He turned back to Clare, his face full of concern. "Are you feeling all right, Miss Caldwell? If there's anything you need—"

"I'm fine," she said quickly. If there was one thing she *didn't* need, it was questions. "Just kind of tired, that's all."

The old man nodded. "Well," he said, "it's been a long day."

"Yes, sir," she agreed. They said good-night then, and Clare started toward the door, but halfway there she turned around. "Mr. Morgan . . . ?"

"Yes, miss?"

"Has there been any—I mean, you haven't heard from Joey—from Joseph yet, have you?"

"No," he said, "not yet." He smiled apologetically. "But I expect it could be any day now."

"I expect so," said Clare.

If wishes were horses, beggars would ride. . . .

She went to the tower room, lay down on the white bed, waited for the line of yellow light to disappear. The curtains were still; not a breath of wind was stirring tonight.

Somewhere in the distant dark a siren wailed.

Clare shivered and thought, *Hyenas.*

20

IT WAS LONG PAST midnight when Clare pushed her way through the broken slat, using her cast as a kind of battering ram.

"What's for supper?" Little Dog asked, relieving her of the shopping bag.

"Three guesses," said Thimble.

"Same as usual," Clare admitted, "plus some apples and crackers and soup for Shoe."

But Shoe seemed to be feeling better tonight.

"Told you all he needed was that pink medicine," Racer said proudly, clapping his patient on the back. "Look at him, good as new. Fever broke a couple hours ago. That's all he needed—just had to sweat it out a little, right, bro?"

Shoe grinned his old grin—or a quieter version of it at least. He was still a bit more subdued than usual, but he really was looking *much* better, Clare thought. His skin was cool to the touch—a little on the clammy side maybe, but there wasn't a smidgen of fever left. And his eyes were bright—glistening like a cat's in the beam from Cowboy's flashlight.

Clare breathed a sigh of relief; that was *one* less worry anyway. She and Little Dog started setting out the food on the concrete block.

But Cowboy's brow was furrowed. "Was there trouble?" he asked her. "You're later than usual."

Clare shrugged. "The old man took his time going to bed, that's all. Fooling around with that crazy plane, I guess." She had decided not to mention Santiago's warning. What good would it do to get the others all worked up? It was her risk, not theirs.

"What about that old plane, Hatso?" Racer asked. "Ain't we ever gonna see it?"

"I don't know," said Clare. She had found the key to the basement door a couple of weeks ago, hanging on a hook inside one of the kitchen cabinets, but she had put off doing anything about it. And now—well, things were shaky enough as it was; there was no sense taking any more chances than they had to.

"Aw, come on, Hatso, what's it gonna hurt? We'll be quiet as little mousies, won't we, Shoe?"

Shoe's eyes grew brighter still, but Cowboy said, "Leave her alone. Hat's doing more than her share already. If she thinks it's risky, we forget it, that's all."

Clare turned to him gratefully. "Maybe later," she said.

Back in the tower room she lay awake, too tired to sleep, listening to the early-morning rain that had just begun to fall. It pattered in and out of her half-dreams, soothed her aching brain. Shoe was better now; maybe everything was going to be okay, after all. Maybe Santiago was only bluffing, maybe the cops would put their suits back on and leave everybody alone, maybe Joey Morgan would call today and tell her to come right out—

You're gonna love it here, kiddo—swimming pools, movie stars, just like they say on TV, you know?

But I've got these friends now, Joey. I can't leave them.

Your friends? No problem. Just bring 'em all with you. I've got plenty of room!

Getting a little carried away here, ain't you, sister? A person could get hurt, pinning all her hopes on a saxophone player.

Go away, Mama. I'm talking to Joey. . . .

But Joey was gone now; the line was dead. Maybe it was the rain. . . . Here was the telephone man now, come to fix it; he was out there on the pole, banging away with his hammer—

Stop it, mister; you're hurting my ears—

But just then the hammering turned to knocking, and Clare's eyes flew open. The rain had stopped, and the sun was shining brightly through the billowing white curtains, and A.J. was knocking and calling to her from the other side of the door:

"Miss Caldwell? Miss Caldwell, I'm sorry to wake you, but there's someone here to see you."

Clare sat up. She was wide awake now, heart pounding, mind racing—was it the police? Had Santiago called them already? "Just a minute," she said, stalling for time, getting out of bed and grabbing her clothes and trying to think what to do. *Is there a back way out of this place?* she wondered, pulling on her shorts.

"Miss Caldwell? I'm so sorry. I told him you were still

sleeping, but—well, it's that Mr. Griffey from the agency, do you remember? He says it's important."

Griffey? Clare froze with one foot half-sneakered. What was he doing here? Had the police called *him?*

"What does he want?"

"I don't know, miss. He didn't explain. He only said that he's spoken to your—to your mother again."

Something turned over inside Clare. *Mama?*

"Miss Caldwell . . . ?"

"All right," she said. "I'm coming."

Griffey was sitting by himself in a corner booth, sipping a soda, glancing through some papers in a manila folder. He looked up as Clare and A.J. came down the spiral staircase. He smiled his sunniest smile.

Okay, Clare thought at him, *you can cool it now, creep, you already won the Oscar.*

"Hello, Clare," he said, standing and holding out his hand.

"Hello," she muttered, ignoring it.

The smile only widened; the hand was unembarrassed; it moved smoothly now, gesturing toward the booth, as if that was what it had intended to do all along. "Have a seat, won't you?"

She sat.

A.J. waved vaguely in the direction of the kitchen. "Should I, ah . . . ?"

"No, no, sit down, Mr. Morgan. No mysteries here." Griffey turned to Clare. "Well, you're looking much better than you were the last time I saw you! Feeling all right now?"

Clare shrugged. "Sure," she said. "I'm fine."

"Glad to hear it. Mr. Morgan's been taking good care of you, I can see that."

168

The old man blushed. "Oh, no. I mean—Miss Caldwell isn't a bit of trouble. She takes care of herself, really."

Griffey nodded. "Of course," he said. "Well, that's wonderful, but I'm sure Clare really appreciates everything you've done."

She wasn't going to sit around all day listening to this bunch of baloney. If there was a point, they might as well get to it. "Mr. Morgan said you talked to my mother."

"Yes," said Griffey. He took a sip of his drink. "As a matter of fact, I did. She called just yesterday."

"She called *you?*"

"Yes," said Griffey. "Does that surprise you?"

Clare felt the blood beating its familiar path to her face. "No," she said. She picked up the saltshaker, twirled it between her fingers. "Why should it?"

"I don't know," said Griffey. He leaned back, crossed his arms.

Clare lowered her eyes. She couldn't stand to see him looking at her that way, as if he were trying to read her mind. "So what's the deal?" she asked.

"I don't know that you'd call it a *deal.*" Clare could feel him smiling at her, willing her to look at him. She didn't. "Your mother has changed her mind, that's all. She misses you, Clare. She wants you to come home."

Silence then, while Griffey let his words sink in. Clare was too surprised to speak. Somehow it was the last thing she had expected.

"We had a long talk," Griffey went on. "She knows there have been problems, but now that she's had some time to think things over, she wants to make a fresh start."

Fresh start? What's that supposed to mean?

The old man was the first to regain his voice. "But doesn't Miss Caldwell—doesn't *she* have something to say? Doesn't your agency want to know what she thinks about all this?"

"Of course we do," said Griffey. His tone was positively greasy with concern. "If there's any reason you wouldn't feel safe at home, Clare—anything you want to tell us, why, now's the time to speak up. No one's forcing you to go back. There are still other alternatives. I think I mentioned them to you before."

Clare suppressed a shudder. She remembered, all right.

"Is there anything about this that—worries you, miss?" The kindness in the old man's voice made Clare's eyes blur with unexpected tears. *What's wrong with you?* she asked herself, blinking them back. *Ain't no way you can tell* him. *No way you can tell anybody.*

She shook her head. "No," she said. She began to push the saltshaker around in a small circle on the table. "I just—" She hesitated.

"Yes, miss?"

"I was just wondering, if Mama—if my mother—is she living by herself now?"

"No," said Griffey. "There's a Mr."—he checked his notes—"a Mr. Sidney Tolliver living there, too. Is that a problem?"

Clare could feel the blood pounding in her throat, her temples, the tips of her ears, feel their four eyes on her, studying her. Six, if you counted Santiago's; he was watching from behind the counter. "No," she said again. "I just—just wondered, is all."

"Well," Griffey said after a moment, "then this is good

news, isn't it? I'll go ahead and make the arrangements, as long as there aren't any objections." He closed the folder, stood up. "Your mother is wiring money for your airline ticket. I'll stop by again tomorrow, give you the game plan, how's that? And in the meantime—"

"In the meantime Miss Caldwell will be fine where she is," said the old man. He sounded defensive for some reason.

"I'm sure she will." Griffey was smiling again. "But I was going to say, in the meantime Clare might want to give her mom a call, talk things over. I think it would be a good idea, don't you, Clare? It's up to you, of course."

Of course, thought Clare. *I just say the secret word, and we all live happily ever after, right?*

She spent the rest of the morning on the beach, staring out at the water, trying to slog through the muddle in her brain. A *fresh start*—had Mama really meant it? Not that it mattered. . . . Though for just a second there, back at the hot-dog palace, a tiny, unreasonable gladness had leapt inside her when Griffey had said those words: *she wants you to come home.* Mama wanted her. It had almost made up for the milk cartons. But there was no way she could go back if Sid was still there. And she wasn't about to go with the red-haired man either. So where did that leave her?

On the moon, that's where.

A mother and her little girl were sitting a little way off, scooping up sand in paper cups to fortify the wall on their castle. Watching them, Clare thought of the first time she had ever seen the ocean. Or not the ocean, really—the Gulf of Mexico was what they had in Biloxi, Mississippi. But it was close enough for jazz, Mama said. She had taken Clare down there on a Memorial Day weekend trip, the summer when Clare was four years old.

Clare hadn't liked it a bit.

"Why on earth not?" Jessie wanted to know. She hadn't driven five hundred sweaty miles in a rented Chevy Nova just to have her kid act like a pill, for heaven's sake. "Come on now, sister. Hold my hand and we'll wade in together."

But Clare had shrunk back, her heart thumping wildly. "It's too full," she tried to explain.

Amazingly, Mama hadn't got mad. She had started to laugh, stopped herself, and then knelt down beside her and hugged her trembling shoulders. "You're right," she said, putting her cheek next to Clare's. "You're absolutely right." And then the two of them had stayed on the shore and made sand castles and gone for ice cream later, and Clare had never been happier.

The memory made her ache. *A fresh start. . . .* She pushed the words out of her head. What good were they? *You blew it, Mama, you missed your chance. It's too late for starting over.* She would run away again, that was all. The hot-dog palace wasn't safe anymore, now that Mama was asking for her. She would have to disappear, take her chances on the boardwalk with the others.

And Joey Morgan? *Quit kidding yourself, kid. It's been a month since you wrote him. He's moved again, or he don't want to write back.* Either way it was too late for him, too. He wasn't going to come sweeping in like Batman or whoever and fix everything. Well, who needed him, anyhow? Clare had other friends, friends she could count on. The gang was the only answer now, wasn't it?

Wasn't it?

You know it's not, came the answer.

What are you talking about, Mama? Ain't nothing else left.

Sure, there is. Something that's been in the back of your mind for a long time, only you wouldn't look at it, would you? Because it scared you more than anything. Because it made you sick, how much it scared you—

No! Don't say it. I couldn't, I can't—

You won't, you mean. Because you're scared. Scared of telling me about Sid. . . .

But you wouldn't understand. You'd say I was lying; you'd think it was my fault—

How do you know? You'll never know for sure if you don't give me a chance. You have to spit it out, sister. You have to say the words.

But I shouldn't have to say them. You should have known, Mama; you should have been paying attention. Mothers are supposed to know things like that. Mothers are supposed to watch out for their kids. . . .

Things like what? Tell me, Clare.

She covered her ears, as if Mama had actually spoken out loud.

The child was crying now; some hairy little creature in a seashell had startled her.

"It's all right, honey," her mother crooned, holding her close. "He won't hurt you."

The words of comfort scratched across Clare's brain like fingernails on a blackboard. She got up and hurried back over the sand. The sun was getting to her, that was all; she was starting to hear voices like old Joan of Arc.

21

CLARE CLIMBED back up the wooden stairs to the board-walk, walked aimlessly for a while, trying to get Mama out of her head. She stopped to listen to a steel band playing from the balcony at Resorts, a man in a clown suit telling jokes on a makeshift stage: "What do you call a fly without wings? A walk! Thank you, sir, thank you. That's the best laugh I've had all day—since before I put on my makeup. . . ."

Good grief. No wonder Atlantic City was dying.

A plump woman in an orange pantsuit was standing on a ladder outside Madame Edna's, tacking up a new sign over the window:

QUESTIONS ABOUT BUSINESS, LOVE, PERSONAL LIFE?
MADAME EDNA HAS THE ANSWERS
WALK IN, BE SEATED, YOU'LL BE GLAD YOU DID
NOW ACCEPTING DINERS CLUB

"Excuse me," she said to Clare, "would you mind handing me that hammer? I got all the way up here, and now I see I've left it behind."

"Sure," Clare said, obliging her.

"Thank you, dear. My legs aren't what they used to be, I'm afraid."

"You're welcome." Clare was about to walk on when the woman said, "You're the young lady staying with A.J., aren't you?" And then, when Clare looked surprised, she added, "I've seen you there a few times, that's all. We go way back, A.J. and I. Oldest neighbors on the boardwalk."

"Oh," said Clare. This was Madame Edna herself, then? She sure didn't *look* much like a fortune-teller.

"Anything I can do for you today?"

"No, thanks," said Clare.

She was halfway to Peanut World when she turned around, retraced her steps. "What've you got for five bucks?" she asked, holding up Joey Morgan's bill. She was sick of it; she wouldn't carry it around another second, as if it were some sacred relic, some chip of a dried-up saint's left shinbone. What was past, was past; this time she really meant it. *Now* was all that mattered, *now* and *now* and *now*.

Madame Edna's face was suddenly dinted with dimples. "Well," she said, climbing down the ladder with surprising agility for a woman of her size, old legs and all, "I'm sure we can work something out."

She ushered Clare inside, relieved her of the money, gestured toward one of a pair of straight-backed chairs beside a small table where a white cat was curled up, sleeping peacefully.

"Move, White Kitty," said the fortune-teller, giving her a gentle push. "She's deaf," Madame Edna explained as the cat stirred and stretched, then took her sweet time moving from the tabletop to her mistress's lap. "But then I'm near-sighted, so we make a good team." She took a pair of glasses from her jacket pocket, put them on. "So, how's the arm? I hear that was a nasty tumble you took."

Good Lord. Does she know my underwear size, too? Clare shrugged. "It's fine," she said. "I'm okay now."

Madame Edna studied her for a moment. "Not so very okay, I think. Too much strain for one so young. Just look at these here." She patted Clare's hands, which were balled into two tight fists on the table before her.

"No," said Clare, making a conscious effort to relax her fingers, "I'm fine, really."

Madame Edna smiled kindly. "If you say so." She pointed to a long crease in the center of Clare's right palm. "Line of life, see there? Running very strong and deep. Then the head line, heart line, line of fate—there and there and there. Oh, yes, good lines, all of them. Very good lines. Are you right-handed, then?"

Some fortune-teller. "Does it matter?" Clare asked.

Madame nodded. "Everyone has two fortunes—the same and not the same."

"*Two* fortunes?"

"One for each hand. The first shows what you're given, you see—what you're born with."

"And the second?"

"That shows what you choose—what you *do* with your gifts. But you have to see both for real understanding, and one of yours is covered." Madame tapped the frayed graying cast.

"So what does that mean? You don't know what I'll do?"

"Only what *you* know already."

"And what's that?"

Madame winked. "Whatever you choose," she said.

Great, thought Clare. *Maybe I ought to choose your career, lady, if you can really make a living with that kind of double-talk.* She stood up. "Well, thanks a lot."

"No, no," said Madame Edna. "Sit down, sweetheart. What's your hurry?"

Clare sat. It wasn't as if she had a bus to catch. "But I thought you said you couldn't tell any more."

"Palms aren't everything," said Madame. She picked up a pack of oversize cards, began shuffling them. The white cat was purring now. "Cut," Madame told Clare, setting the cards on the table. "As many times as you like."

Clare did as she was told, making a very deep cut first, then a shallow one, for no particular reason. Madame nodded again, then picked up the cards and began laying them out on the table in a peculiar design that Clare could make neither heads nor tails of. Some complicated game of solitaire, it appeared, except that these cards were nothing like any deck she had ever seen before: they were all pictures—some pretty, some downright creepy—not just the normal kings and queens and jacks but a skeleton in a black robe and a hanged man and a big-bosomed lady pouring wine from one goblet to another; sort of reminded Clare of Mama, come to think of it—

"The cups of love are not yet full," said Madame Edna, speaking as she dealt. "I see anger and confusion. But there is pride, too, and great promise. See the emperor on his throne?"

More double-talk, thought Clare. She was just about to get up again when Madame Edna said, "Don't expect too much of your friend Joe."

Clare's head jerked up. "You saw that in the cards?"

Madame kept dealing. "I've known the Morgans for a long time, that's all. And Joe . . . We were friends, too, many years ago. He used to come and talk to me, before he ran away."

"*Why* did he run away?" Clare asked. Not that she cared anymore; still, as long as she was here . . .

Madame Edna shook her head. "He was sixteen when his mother left—just about broke his heart, poor boy. He went after her—followed her to New York City. But he wasn't happy there either. He wouldn't have been happy anywhere in those days. So of course they quarreled, and then he ran away for good."

"His mother *left*? But I thought—I mean, I saw pictures—all of 'em smiling, sitting in that crazy plane."

Madame sighed, turned over a card with a curly-tailed devil. "The plane," she repeated. "I've told A.J. a thousand times, he ought to sell it, give it to a museum. He almost lost an eye to that plane, did you know? Some sort of welding accident. . . . He keeps it perfect, ready to fly but never flying. 'Waiting for what?' I ask him. 'They're not coming back, A.J. Sell it and forget the past. Those days are gone.' But does he listen? He makes himself sick, grieving for what is lost."

Clare thought this over for a moment, then asked, "But wasn't it his own fault that he lost it? He must've done something to make them leave."

Madame smiled, shook her head again. "Young Joe used to talk of fault. His father's fault for not seeing that his wife was unhappy, his mother's fault for not loving enough. It was no one's fault, everyone's fault. Only God is perfect, and Him I don't understand. Just look who He gets to run the country!"

"You mean—there ain't nothing else? Nothing the old man's hiding? I mean, he *seems* nice and all, but—"

Madame chuckled. "Contrary to popular opinion, my dear, sometimes people *are* what they seem." She turned over another card. "Oh, my, look at this."

"What?"

"The card—see there?"

"What's it mean?"

"What do *you* think it means?"

What a gyp. Clare shrugged. "I don't know—looks like a couple of roads coming together."

"Exactly." Madame beamed at her. "You're at a crossroads, don't you see? One path leads one way, one leads another. Only you can decide which you'll take."

"How do I know which is the right one?"

"You don't," said Madame Edna. "That's the tricky part."

"Hey, look at all this!" Little Dog exclaimed. "Four packages of hot dogs and three times as much chili as usual and soup and crackers and pickles and apples and what's under the tinfoil?"

"A chocolate pie," said Clare. Santiago had baked a pair of them today and he was bound to notice, but what would it matter after tonight? she had figured.

"Chocolate?" Even Thimble was impressed. "What's the occasion?"

Clare reached in her shorts pocket, pulled out a set of keys. "Y'all still want to see that old plane?"

□   □   □

They slipped through the front door one at a time, moving shadows, nothing more. Made their way noiselessly past the dark counter, the silent soda wheel, the tables with their chairs upended.

"Look like dead spiders," Racer whispered.

"Shh," she warned him, sliding the key into the lock on the basement door, turning it quietly. The cellar yawned before them, black as sin. "Careful now." One by one they passed her, holding tightly to the wooden railing, easing down the stairs into the darkness below. And when they were all through, she closed the door behind her and flipped on the light.

"Oh, man!" Racer kept whispering, as he circled the strange silver bird. "Oh man oh man oh man!" For once he was almost as wordless as Shoe, who was too awestruck to giggle, even; he just stood and gaped, scarcely breathing, it appeared, while Thimble leaned against the bottom of the stair railing with her arms crossed, looking pointedly bored, and Racer kept quietly circling, making little gasping sounds as he came upon each new marvel: "Wow!" and "Cool!" and "Man oh man oh *man!*"

Little Dog's eyes were shining, too, though he tried not to show it. "Not bad," he said, as if he had seen dozens of better homemade aeroplanes in other basements. "Not bad at all." He peered into the cockpit. "It really works?"

"That's what the old man says," said Clare.

"Sure it does," said Racer. "I seen this same kind of plane in *The Great Waldo Pepper*—old Robert Redford, remember? Shoot, wish I knew how—I'd fly it outa here right now. Wouldn't that be something? *Whoosh!* I'm gone!"

180

"What was this place anyhow?" Little Dog asked, looking around the enormous room. "Couldn't've been built just for hot dogs."

"Used to be a movie house," Clare explained. "A.J. says his folks ran it till they died. Then he took it over. But when TV came along people didn't go to movies as much. So he had to turn it into a restaurant."

"Aw, man." Racer shook his head. "Old TV—ain't that the pits?"

Shoe turned his burning eyes on Clare, pointed to the pilot's seat.

"He wants to know can he sit in there," Racer explained.

"Sure," said Clare. As long as she had gone this far. "Why not?"

A moment later Shoe was perched above her, peering down through a crazy-looking pair of flying goggles that he had found hanging by the controls. Grinning like mad.

"Look at Shoe—he's a ace!" Racer whispered, clambering up behind him to the first of the two sets of passenger seats. "Come on, you guys—there's room for everybody!"

Room for a whole family, the old man had said. . . .

Little Dog smiled and pulled Thimble along with him— "This is so dumb," she muttered—and the two of them joined the others in the plane. But Clare and Cowboy held back for a while, stood watching the pure joy glowing in Shoe's grimy little face, the laughter in Racer's as he pounded the new arrivals on the back and flashed Cowboy the thumbs-up signal. . . .

"Something's happened, hasn't it?" Cowboy asked quietly.

Clare took a deep breath, let it out slowly. "I can't stay here no more, that's all."

"That guy—the one you were waiting for—he never showed?"

She shrugged. "It don't matter. I can't hardly remember what he looks like."

"Finks," Cowboy muttered, shaking his head. "Can't trust any of 'em." He gave Clare's shoulder a brotherly pat. "Don't sweat it, Hat. You're with us now."

Clare swallowed hard; her throat was giving her trouble again. "But the food—we need it. I won't be able to get it after this."

"Forget the food. We'll make out. We always do, right? Crackdown won't last forever. L.D. was saying just yesterday he thought it was already easing up some."

Thimble was eyeing them narrowly from the backseat. "So what are you two whispering about? You coming up here or what?"

"Sure," said Cowboy. "Come on, Hat." And he gave Clare a boost over the plane's silver side and started to climb in after her—

But just then there was the unmistakable sound of footsteps in the room overhead.

"It's the old man!" Clare whispered. "Quick! Everybody out!"

And then there was a frantic scrambling and scurrying, while Clare ran to the far wall and flipped the secret switch. *Thanks, Joey,* she thought, as the magic wall hummed to life and the gang hurtled through. *Thanks for that much, anyway.*

"Who's there?" came A.J.'s voice from the top of the stairs. "Miss Caldwell, is that you?"

No, she thought back at him, *Miss Caldwell's long gone.*

She flipped the switch once more, then followed her friends into the night. "Good-bye, Joey Morgan. Good-bye, old man. See you on the moon," she whispered as the door slammed shut behind her.

22

But the moon was smelling more like green cheese every day. L.D. had been mistaken about the crackdown easing up. You could spot them on every corner, practically—shifty-eyed cops in their ill-fitting store-bought clothes, trying to blend in with the ordinary tourists. Of course some of the tourists were pretty shifty-eyed themselves, so you could never be *absolutely* certain. Which meant that before long the gang was running from their own shadows, balking at hits that would have been easy pickings earlier in the summer. It got so bad they had to resort to scams they would have considered beneath them in ordinary times.

"It's not so terrible," Little Dog explained to Clare as they stood beside a pay phone one night. "I just call up the pizza place, see?" he said, dialing as he spoke. "And then when they answer I give 'em this number and tell 'em we're coming to pick it up, get it? Yeah, this is Ed. I want two extralarge pizzas with everything but the fish, got that? How

184

much? No, no problem. How long before we can pick it up? Okay, see you in twenty minutes."

"What'd he say?" Clare asked, when Little Dog had hung up.

"He said twenty-one dollars and eighty-seven cents, be ready in twenty minutes."

"But we ain't got twenty-one eighty-seven."

L.D. grinned. "We don't need it."

"But how . . . ?"

"We just hang loose for a while, that's all. Pizza place closes in an hour, right? That's when they throw out all the pies nobody's come for—put 'em in that Dumpster around back."

Clare's mouth dropped open. "We're gonna eat pizza out of a *Dumpster*?"

"There's nothing wrong with it. We just take the fresh ones, that's all. Boxed up nice and neat—prob'ly find the ones we ordered, even."

It worked pretty well, too, as long as you didn't *think* about it too hard. For a whole week they took turns making the calls, until Little Dog got into a fight with a bum who had the same idea. L.D. ended up with a bloody nose and a whole slew of bruises, and nobody had any supper that night.

And then Shoe got sick again.

Or maybe it wasn't so much *again*; Clare suspected he had never really got well from the first time—or from farther back than that, even, now that she thought about it. All that toilet flushing—that wasn't just a hobby, was it? And when was it she had first noticed him living on air? Anyway, no matter how long it had been going on, there wasn't any ignoring it now; even Racer's doses of pink medicine weren't doing any good anymore.

"There's stronger stuff behind the counter," said Racer, "if we could just get to it."

"No way," said Cowboy. "They know us in there, remember? We can't even get in the door anymore, much less behind the counter."

"So we hit it at night," said Racer. "After they close. Old Ginger won't be around then."

"You mean break in?" Clare asked. "How? They got burglar alarms, don't they?"

"It's too risky," said Cowboy. "We'll have to buy the medicine, that's all. Get the money someplace else."

"Where?" Racer wanted to know. "Ain't nothing safe these days. Ketchup caper's no good with Shoe sick. Ain't nobody else fast enough."

"He needs a doctor," said Thimble, frowning and rubbing his skinny arms. "Look how he's shivering."

Racer took off his own skimpy jacket, wrapped it around Shoe's shoulders. "He's cold, that's all. Turning to winter early this year."

It was true; the first September norther had blown in that morning, leaving the air crisp and cool: football weather, Mama would have called it. It would have been fine on a starry night in a stadium, tucked up under a blanket maybe, with a cup of hot chocolate. But it wasn't so great in the drafty old garage.

"We'll move back to Baltic as soon as Shoe can make it," said Cowboy. "It stays a little warmer there, away from the beach."

"What he needs is a couple nights in a real bed," said Little Dog, shaking his head over his notebook. "But we don't have money for a motel."

"So we'll get it," said Cowboy. He was pacing again. "Enough to last us a while this time."

"How?" Thimble asked.

"I don't know," said Cowboy. "I'm thinking."

"Might as well hit the drugstore, then," Racer suggested again. "Plenty money in there."

"No," said Little Dog, "they put it in a safe at night— no way you could touch it."

"Don't matter—there's all that other stuff—watches, jewelry—we could get to that. Pick up the medicine on the same trip."

"*Forget* the drugstore." Cowboy's voice was sharp. "I told you, it's too dangerous."

Racer held his tongue after that, but nobody came up with any brighter ideas, though Cowboy paced and worried all afternoon. One after another was trotted out and rejected: Captain Billy had posted a twenty-four-hour watchman at the Trash 'n Treasure; there were undercover cops patrolling the Dixieland concerts at Brighton Park; Thimble had been recognized trying to slip past the guard to play the quarter slots at Bally's. Even the ticket taker at the Super-Loops had begun to look suspicious when one of the gang got too close to his till. And meantime Shoe had to make so many trips to the bathroom at Burger World that the manager noticed and asked him to leave, and every time he returned to the garage the circles under his eyes looked a little deeper, a shade or two darker. . . .

"Come on, Hatso," Racer said just before sundown, "let's take us a walk."

"Where are you guys going?" Little Dog asked.

"Gonna check out the old ladies coming outa Rodney

Dangerfield," said Racer. "Bound to find a couple soft touches with Hatso in this cast."

"What do you mean?" Clare asked, drawing back. "We ain't gonna *beg*!"

"Naw," said Racer. "We'll sell a couple lucky numbers, that's all."

"Just be careful," Cowboy called after them.

But they never went near the old ladies.

"Looky there," said Racer, slowing down just outside the Rexall. "Old Ginger's getting ready to go home, ain't she?"

Clare glanced through the window. The waitress was wiping off the counter where Clare had eaten French toast a million years ago, straightening the little salt-pepper-sugar-ketchup-napkin islands, glancing at her watch as her last customer finished his sandwich and coffee.

"So what if she is? Don't mean nothing to us. Cowboy said—"

"Aw, man, don't know what's wrong with Cowboy lately. Never seen him so jumpy. Do me a favor, Hatso; keep a lookout, will you? I got an errand to run."

"What kind of errand?"

"Gonna hang out in their rest room till they're gone, that's all, then pick up a couple things and slide out the back window. You can open it easy from the inside."

"No, Racer, don't do it—"

But he was already moving toward the door. Ginger had left her station to help the cashier steady a large cardboard cutout of a blond in a bikini who was selling mouthwash or some such; their backs were turned for the moment. "Just keep a lookout, Hatso," he said, shaking her off when she tried to grab his arm. "I'll be back before you know it."

And then he was gone, and there was nothing she could do but stand there watching from across the boardwalk while he slipped through the door and disappeared somewhere between the paper diapers and the wrinkle removers.

Clare held her breath while a minute passed, then two, three. . . . He must be in the bathroom by this time, surely. Ginger and the cashier were still struggling with the cardboard blond; they made no sign that they had seen him.

Five, six, seven and a half . . . The sandwich eater was leaving now. The cashier locked the door and shook his head at a lady who came rushing up at the last second. *No, Clare could see him mouthing, we're closed. Right*, she thought, *ain't no time for fooling around. Let's just get this over with.*

But another half hour ticked by while Ginger and the cashier plodded about their final business, tallying receipts, straightening shelves, picking up magazines that had been thumbed through and misplaced on the magazine racks. *Just don't check the bathroom*, Clare prayed, picturing Racer standing on the toilet seat, holding his breath. . . .

They didn't, for a wonder. At last Ginger hung up her apron, put on her coat, walked to the Out door with the cashier. He stopped to turn off the lights, leaving only the usual security bulbs burning, then used his key again to get outside. Clare remembered herself as they stepped onto the boardwalk; she bent down over her shoe, pretending to fiddle with the laces. Neither adult paid any attention to her. Ginger laughed at some remark the cashier had made; they said good-night, walked off in opposite directions.

Thank the Lord, Clare thought, breathing again. *Now come on, Racer. Get the stuff and get out of there.*

But he waited, of course. That only made sense; what

if the cashier had remembered something when he was a block away and turned back? *Another* half hour passed—or it might have been a year. The sea and the sky grew dark, and the island put on its nighttime sparkle, and Clare shivered a little as the wind kicked up; her shorts were all wrong for September.

Come on, *Racer!* She wondered if she should run to the hideout, tell Cowboy what was going on. It would be better to have the others here in case anything went wrong, wouldn't it? But she decided not to chance it; Racer had asked her to be his lookout—if anyone started coming, it would be up to her to let him know somehow. She stuck to her post, glancing nervously up and down the boardwalk, trying to size up every passerby. Was that a cop—that tall guy with the skimpy beard and the Mount Rushmore T-shirt? What about the too-cool dude in the leather jacket, the chubby lady cracking her gum? *Cripes*, everybody looked suspicious tonight. . . .

Suddenly she saw Racer—just a shadow, really—inside the Rexall, darting past the panty hose and the athlete's-foot powder, disappearing behind the prescription counter, appearing again a moment later at the *window*, for crying out loud; there he was, posing with Shoe's new medicine like some guy in a commercial—a grinning face next to the cardboard blond. *Are you crazy?* Clare mouthed at him. *Get outa there, man!* But he only winked and disappeared once more. *He's going after the watches now*, Clare thought helplessly. *But the case'll be locked. Did you think of that, Racer?*

A muffled crashing noise from inside was her answer— breaking glass? *No, man—not that way—they got alarms on those things!*

It started in the same heartbeat—the most god-awful

racket she had ever heard. Clare flew to the window and caught sight of Racer at the cracked display case, still frantically stuffing his pockets with watches. "Get outa there, Racer!" she hollered, banging on the window and waving wildly. "They're coming—can't you hear?" Already she could see dark shapes rushing toward her on the boardwalk from both directions. She waited only long enough to see Racer heading to the bathroom; then she started running. She had to get around to the back to make sure he made it out that window he had told her about. . . .

But the drugstore was smack up against its neighbors on the left and right; there was no *way* to get around. She had to run clear to North Carolina Avenue, then duck through a series of alleys and side streets, panicking every step of the way: *Come on, Racer, move it, man—you oughta be outa there by now!* She paused, confused; everything looked different from back here. There was only one long stretch of graffiti-scrawled brick and mortar, with doors and windows scattered at odd intervals. Which one of these buildings was the drugstore, anyway? Was she even in the right block? Or maybe Racer had got out already; maybe he was on his way back to the hideout—

All at once there was the sound of more glass breaking, and she turned and saw him—his legs first, kicking their way through a small window that was maybe thirty yards from where she was standing; it hadn't been so easy to open, then. And now the rest of him, climbing out, leaping to the ground.

"Racer!" she hollered. "This way!"

He saw her then and started toward her, but he hadn't taken two steps before a blue-shirted cop was coming through the window after him.

"Run!" Clare shouted; he could still get away, couldn't he? No cop was as fast as he was—

Only suddenly there wasn't just one cop; here was another, bursting through the back of the building next door, shining his flashlight in Racer's face and—*good Lord*, were those *guns* they were pointing at him?

"No! Leave him alone!" The words tumbled out before she could stop them; now they were all looking at her.

"Get outa here, Hat!" Racer yelled; he was frozen, his hands in the air.

And now one of the policemen was starting in her direction, and for a second she was frozen, too, watching him come—

Until something clicked inside her and her legs sprang to life and she was running again, running like the wind, like a fox with a pack of hungry bloodhounds on its tail, flying back the way she had come, as best as she could remember, through alleys and side streets; running blindly, as she had run in nightmares, with terror in her craw and the wind like needles in her lungs and a jumble of voices crying out in her head: *Maybe you should've—? What will they ever—? Racer, oh, Racer, oh, Racer, you dummy!*

23

"THEY GOT HIM," she panted, bursting through the broken slat. "They got Racer."

The others were around her almost before the words left her mouth.

"Who got him?" asked Cowboy.

"The cops—at the drugstore." The story came pouring out then, in gasps and sobs and hiccups, while Shoe's eyes grew wide with worry and Cowboy's face darkened dangerously.

"Why didn't you stop him?" Thimble asked sharply. "Why didn't you come for us *before* they caught him?"

"I tried to—I told him not to do it, but he wouldn't listen."

Cowboy said nothing, just stood there for a moment, fists clenched, eyes blazing, while Clare fumbled through her explanations. And then he turned abruptly and started walking toward the shafts of light falling through the fence from the streetlamp outside.

The others ran after him.

"Where are you going?" Little Dog asked. "There's nothing we can do now."

"We'll see," Cowboy muttered. "You guys wait here."

"No," said Thimble. "I'm going with you."

"Me, too," Clare and Little Dog said together, and then Clare added, "We got to stick together. That's how Racer got in trouble, going off on his own."

Shoe was following, too.

"No," Cowboy told him, putting a gentle hand on his shoulder. "You're sick, buddy. You stay here. I'll take care of Racer."

But Shoe only shook his head stubbornly; Cowboy might just as well have tried telling him to give up breathing.

He was silent then, looking around him at the circle of anxious faces. "All right, then," he growled at last. "If you're coming, come on."

They spent the rest of the night huddled under a tarp in the back of an old pickup truck that somebody had left parked on a side street half a block from the police station. A quadruple set of parking tickets was stuck under one of its rusting windshield wipers.

From here they could see the station door.

"You think he's in there?" Clare whispered.

"He's there," Cowboy answered.

She knew better than to ask how he could be so certain.

"So what's the plan?" Little Dog asked.

Cowboy shrugged. "There is no plan. We wait, that's all. Play it by ear."

And so they waited, staying close together for warmth, making themselves as comfortable as they could on the hard-bottomed truck bed amid the assorted junk the owner had piled there: dirt-encrusted garden tools and broken flowerpots and rusting stakes. A gardener's truck, then—that was what this was. And after a while their eyes grew heavy, and one by one they gave way to exhaustion and slept—all but Cowboy, anyway.

Clare tried to fight it. *Watch and pray*—the words floated up from the bottom of her memory—*that you may not enter into temptation. . . .* She wanted to be ready if something happened. But the soft snoring of the others lulled her, or maybe there wasn't enough oxygen under the tarp, or possibly she was just flat worn out; whatever the reason, after a while her eyes closed, and she dreamed she was being chased again: she was running down the boardwalk, trying to get to the tower room. She could see it just ahead; it had grown impossibly tall somehow, and Madame Edna was leaning out the window, waving to her: "Jump!" she called down. "Jump or they'll get you!"

"I can't!" Clare called back. "It's too high."

"But this is only a dream," Madame Edna explained. "You can fly if you want to."

And so Clare spread her arms like wings and leapt into the air, but it didn't work; even in the dream that she knew was a dream she was too heavy, gravity was too strong—it pulled her right back down. And now her pursuers were closing in from the surrounding darkness—cops? No, not cops—not human, even. What was that terrible sound they were making? Worse than wolves—a kind of unearthly laughter, it was: snarling, howling, *yip yap yowlll*ing—

"No!" she said aloud, jerking awake.

"It's okay, Hat," Cowboy whispered, shaking her shoulder. "You're dreaming, that's all."

"Oh," she murmured. She was quiet for a moment, waiting for her heart to slow down. The others were still asleep. Shoe moaned a little, tossed off Little Dog's elbow, which must have been cutting into his ribs, then settled down again, his face wet from a mixture of sweat and tears, his nearly weightless frame reeking of dirt and sickness. They all looked half-sick in the dim yellow light trickling in from the streetlamp, didn't they? Thimble with her bad teeth and skinny little Shoe, and even Little Dog had begun to lose weight lately. His skin didn't look all that good either; it had a slack pastiness about it that couldn't have been healthy. And Cowboy—well, he seemed all right at first glance, but there were always heavy circles under the brown eyes, circles the color of bruises; Clare didn't think he ever slept very well. . . .

He was still awake now, leaning up against the spare tire, staring out through the crack between the tarp and the side of the truck. Keeping an eye on the station door, even at this unlikely hour: watching out for his friend.

"What'll they do with him?" Clare asked quietly.

Cowboy took a deep breath, let it out slowly. "He's just a kid," he said, "and he was unarmed. But it was breaking and entering. . . . They'll have him up before a juvenile court officer in the morning, probably. And then—" He hesitated.

"Then what?"

"Then we'll see," said Cowboy. "Could be a lot of things, depending on his record. And how much room they have in their detention homes. And what the judge ate for breakfast, maybe. Those guys are all different. You never know what you're gonna get."

Clare was quiet for a moment, thinking this over. At last she said, "Do you think they'll call Griffey?"

Cowboy gave her a long, searching look. They had never discussed the red-haired man since that long-ago day on the boardwalk. "I don't know," he said finally, turning his eyes back to the station door. "Maybe."

Another silence. And then the question wouldn't stay in Clare's throat any longer: "Is that what happened to you?"

This time Cowboy waited so long to answer that she gave up hoping he would. When he spoke again his voice almost startled her. "I was fourteen when I left home," he said, so quietly that she had to lean in to catch his words. "About Racer's age, I guess. My dad and I—we didn't get along, you know? The way he treated my mom—I wouldn't stand for it, that's all. I mean, even when I was a kid, I would try to fight him. But he was a big guy—must've weighed close to two hundred and fifty pounds. There wasn't anything I could do back then. And my mom—" Cowboy hesitated, made a small, bitter exhaling noise. "She always took his side," he went on. "She'd be standing there with both her eyes black, bruises all over, and she'd say, 'Stop it, Warren. You don't understand—it was my fault.' " Cowboy shook his head. "Her fault. Her fault for marrying the jerk maybe, her fault for staying with him, that's all. She never hurt anybody in her life. But him—he broke her nose once; that's the kind of guy he was. I was eleven. I called the cops that time. But she lied to them, said it was just an accident—she had slipped on some ice in the driveway, fallen funny. And they bought it, those clowns—can you

197

believe it? Or maybe they didn't. They went away, that's all I know. . . ."

Cowboy paused, picked up one of the old flowerpots, starting absently clearing out an ancient spiderweb inside.

"Is she still with him?" Clare asked, after a moment.

Cowboy didn't answer right away. Then, "No," he said softly. "She's dead. They said it was cancer. Sure, she smoked and all; I'm not saying she wasn't weak. But it was him that killed her, same's if he'd put a gun to her head. Dying was the only way she could get out." Cowboy shook his head. "He actually had the nerve to cry at her funeral." He paused once more, and then he added, "I fought him again that night. I was bigger by then, had him worried at least. But there wasn't any reason for me to hang around after that."

"So you left."

Cowboy nodded. "Mom and I—we used to come to Atlantic City in the summers sometimes. We didn't live far from here. I always liked it. But this time—I didn't have any idea what I was doing, just winging it, you know? Made some bonehead moves, like Racer—got picked up once or twice. That was when I met Griffey. . . ."

Cowboy had the web wrapped around his finger now. He studied it for a moment. "I thought he was a great guy, at first. Nothing like my dad. He seemed—like the kind of person you could really count on, you know? You wouldn't believe it—how funny he can be. And how he listens— makes you feel like *somebody*. No one ever made me feel like that before. Like I mattered, I mean. Like he cared. That's why he's dangerous, because at first you think—that's all it is. He's just—showing affection, you know? And this is how it's *supposed* to be, when someone really cares about you. Because we're all just like—his kids—his best friends in the world. One big happy family. . . ."

Cowboy hesitated, then plowed on; it was as if the words wouldn't stop, now that they had started. "And then one day he brings around some other friends. They can help us out, too, he tells us. They've got money, these guys. They want to spread it around. But they're lonely; they need people to be nice to them—to have fun with, that's all. They're just looking for a little fun. . . ." That bitter exhaling sound again. "I was so dense, I *still* didn't get it. Bought everything he was selling. Only it turned out what he was selling was us." Cowboy started wiping the remains of the spiderweb on his jeans. "They said it was a party, gave us wine and crud. Wasn't until I woke up the next day that I understood what had happened. And knew the truth about Griffey."

"The truth . . . ?"

Another pause. And then Cowboy said quietly, "That he wasn't so different from my old man, after all."

Clare felt sick. A whole ocean of pink medicine couldn't have cured the sickness she felt. She was silent for a while, fighting it. And then she asked, because she had to know, "Did you ever—tell anybody? Someone who could stop him, I mean?"

Cowboy shook his head. "It's my word against his. Who'd believe me?"

Clare didn't answer. What was the point?

They were quiet for a long time then—hours, maybe; Clare couldn't have said. But sleep never came near her again. And finally in the first faint light of dawn the others began to stir. Shoe was aching, so they took turns taking him to whatever bathrooms they could find. On her trip

Thimble went to the nearest Dairy Delite and picked up a pretty good bag of leftovers from some family with eyes bigger than its stomach: a couple of halves of ham and egg biscuit, an only slightly watery strawberry shake—enough to keep everybody going for a while, anyway.

There were people out and about now, on their way to work—passing on the sidewalks, driving by in their cars, trying to find parking spaces.

"Be ready to run if the truck driver comes," Cowboy warned the others. But nobody showed up; nobody bothered them even as the morning wore on.

"How long do we wait?" Little Dog asked.

"As long as it takes," Cowboy answered.

"But what if they take him out through the back or something?" Thimble asked. "What if—"

"Shh!" Cowboy put a hand up; he was peering through the crack in the tarp once more.

"What is it?" Clare whispered, and they all leaned in, trying to see.

It was Griffey, red hair ablaze in the morning sun, striding up the sidewalk as if he owned it. Stopping to speak briefly to a pretty lady walking the other way, to wave at a fellow across the street. Griffey waited for this guy, shook hands when he caught up. They walked up the station steps together, laughing about something that Griffey had said.

"You think he's there for Racer?" Thimble asked. Clare gave her a look; Thimble knew about Griffey, too, then? How many had he hurt?

"Maybe" was all Cowboy said, as the two men disappeared inside the building.

An hour passed. Or maybe it was less, but it *seemed* longer. There was no way of knowing; Racer was the one with the watches, Clare thought bitterly. And then just when Shoe had started to squirm and Little Dog was about to take him on another bathroom run, the door opened again.

"Perfect," Cowboy breathed.

It was Griffey again, with Racer beside him. Just the two of them, walking toward the side street; Racer wasn't cuffed or bound in any way, unless you counted Griffey's hand on his shoulder—only a friendly guiding pressure, it looked like. But Clare remembered its peculiar strength. . . .

At the sight of his friend, Shoe made an inarticulate sound—something between a sob and a shout for joy—and would have gone after him if Cowboy hadn't held him back. "No," he whispered. "Wait till they get past us."

And so they *waited*—one Mississippi, two Mississippi, three Mississippi, four . . .

Griffey was turning the corner now; he and Racer were about twenty yards away, with their backs to the truck.

"Okay," said Cowboy. "I'll get Racer. You guys go on to the Baltic house. We'll meet you there."

"No," said Thimble. "We're coming with you."

"You heard me," Cowboy said. "There's no time to argue."

He was climbing out of the truck already, shadowing Griffey and Racer on the sidewalk. Clare and Thimble waited maybe thirty seconds, then looked at each other and started after him. No way were they going to leave him to battle that creep alone.

"Wait up!" said Little Dog, following with Shoe.

Griffey and Racer were stopping now beside a car—a shiny little foreign job. Griffey reached in his pocket for his keys, said something to Racer, smiled his million-dollar smile. Racer didn't answer. Griffey didn't seem to mind; he unlocked the door on the passenger side, leaned over to open it for Racer . . .

"Forget it, Griffey," Cowboy said, grabbing him in a choke hold from behind.

Racer wheeled around, his face alight. "Hey, Cowboy," he said. "I knew you'd come!"

"Go on, get outa here," Cowboy told him, and Racer ran and joined the others, who were forming a semicircle around Griffey and Cowboy, blocking them from the street. There were no cars passing at the moment, but you never knew.

"Don't do this, Warren." Griffey's voice was calm, confident, even now, when Cowboy could have broken his neck if he wanted to. "This boy is in trouble. I can help him."

"Sure," said Cowboy. "The way you helped me, right?"

"You'll never get away with it. The island's not big enough. We know where to find you, Warren."

"I'll take my chances."

Griffey's eyes fell on Clare. "Well, hello, Miss Caldwell," he said, as cordially as if they had just met at a church picnic. "We wondered where you were keeping yourself."

There it was again—that wave of sickness. . . . If it were really possible for blood to run cold, Clare's was doing it now.

Cowboy tightened his grip. "Shut up, Griffey," he said. He looked at the others. "So move it, you guys. What are you waiting for?"

And now they were running, running for their lives, whisking Shoe along with them—though no one was chasing them; not even Griffey, when Cowboy let him go and followed his friends. Clare glanced back over her shoulder and saw the red-haired man standing beside his car still, watching them. Why should he work up a sweat? she could feel him thinking. It was six to one; those weren't the odds he would choose. He would go back to the police station, get all the help he wanted. And then he would come after them.

We know where to find you. . . .

24

THEY RAN all the way to Baltic, tumbled through the boarded-up window, breathless and shaking, only to be met by muffled screams. A homeless family had set up housekeeping inside—a pregnant mother and her gaunt-looking husband and two pretty little girls of maybe three and four, who started to cry and cling to their father's trousers when Cowboy and the others came bursting inside.

"This is *our* place," said Little Dog, pulling his notebook out of his pocket. "We were here first. I can prove it—I've got records."

"We don't want trouble," said the man. "This is all—new to us. We'll move on. Just don't—don't try anything. We've got nothing you'd want."

He's scared to death, thought Clare.

Cowboy stood quietly for a minute, studying them, still catching his breath. "How long have you been out of work?" he asked finally.

The man seemed embarrassed. "That's none of your—" he began, and then he paused and said, "A while. About a year."

For a moment Clare wondered if Cowboy was going to invite them all to join the gang. Four and a half new members; there wouldn't be names enough, would there? But the prospect must have seemed overwhelming, even to him, with Griffey's threats still warm in his ears. And so after another minute had passed, he shrugged and said, "Forget it. You can have the place. We're leaving town anyway."

"What?" Thimble grabbed his arm. "What do you mean, leaving town? Leaving the *boardwalk?*"

"You heard me," he said. "Come on, you guys." He turned to go, but the woman stepped up to him, cleared her throat.

"There are a few—things here. Maybe they're yours? Games and things." She pointed to the rickety kitchen table, where the old Monopoly board was lying open.

Cowboy looked at it for a moment. Then he shook his head. "Keep it," he said. He turned to leave, but halfway to the window he hesitated, came back toward the woman. "You can't really—" he began, reaching in his pocket with his right hand.

But before he could complete the motion, the man lunged at him—so quickly that Clare didn't understand what was happening. She saw Cowboy's face change—his eyes widen in disbelief, his mouth drop open—and heard his sudden sharp intake of breath; it sounded as if he had had the wind knocked out of him.

The others seemed just as confused as she was. "Cowboy?" Thimble said uncertainly, and Little Dog and Racer moved in protectively, but Cowboy shook his head at them, held up his left hand, and they stopped just as the man stepped back—or *staggered* back; that was more like it. His face was white, as startled as Cowboy's.

He was holding a knife.

"I told you not to try anything," he said. His voice and knife hand were both shaking.

For a second no one moved. Then slowly, carefully, so as not to spook him any further, Cowboy took his right hand the rest of the way out of his pocket, held it open for the man to see. In his palm were a pair of dice and the old playing pieces: horseback rider for Cowboy, car for Racer, little dog, thimble, shoe, and a small silver hat. . . .

"I was going to say, you can't really play without these."

"Oh, God," said the man. He was shaking all over now, fighting tears. "Oh, my God, kid, I'm sorry. I thought you had a gun; I thought you were going to—" He broke off, as if he were choking on his own words. The knife fell from his hand, clattered onto the scarred linoleum.

Little Dog started to go for it.

"No." Cowboy's voice brought him up short. "Leave it," he said. He was still holding out the tokens. One of the little girls stepped up boldly and took them from him, then ran to the safety of her mother's legs and peeped out from behind them, smiling.

Cowboy smiled back at her—an odd little half-smile. "Okay," he said. "Let's get out of here."

They were two blocks away before Clare saw the blood.

It was dripping from the left cuff of his blue jeans, running down the side of his sneaker, leaving bloody footprints on the sidewalk behind them.

"Good Lord, Cowboy, you're hurt!" she cried.

He shook his head, kept walking. "It's nothing," he said. "I can hardly feel it."

"But you're bleeding! You ought to go to a hospital—"

"No!" He almost shouted it. "No hospitals," he said, a little more quietly. "I'll be fine once we get back to the garage. I just need to rest awhile, that's all." He staggered a little. Thimble and Little Dog each put an arm around him, and they continued, traveling in a zigzag pattern again, avoiding the busier streets, shying away from curious glances—of which there were surprisingly few; it was almost as if the kids were invisible except to one another.

Halfway there Cowboy had to stop. He leaned over and spit blood into the gutter.

"This is crazy," said Clare, trying to keep the panic out of her voice. "We ain't got a choice. We *have* to take him to a hospital."

"No hospitals." Cowboy still shook his head stubbornly, though now there was blood oozing out from under his clenched left fist, which he was holding fast against his side. "They'd call the police. Griffey'd be there in five minutes. He's right; the island's too small."

"So we'll get off the island," said Clare. "We'll go somewhere else."

"*How?*" asked Little Dog. "We can't walk—they could be watching the bridges. And we don't have money for bus tickets."

"We could hitch," Racer suggested.

"No way," said Thimble. "All *six* of us? Standing by the highway with our thumbs out? Cops'd be sure to see us then."

"What else is there?" Little Dog asked. "We don't have a boat. What are we supposed to do—fly?"

Cowboy sat down heavily on the sidewalk. "You guys go on," he said. "I'll catch up later. I just have to rest a minute."

"Forget it," said Thimble, pulling him to his feet. "We stick together. That's the rule, remember?" She sounded angry, but her eyes were bright with tears.

"There's gotta be *something* we can do," said Clare, casting about frantically in her mind. "A church—they wouldn't have to call the cops, would they? Ain't there some rule about sanctuary? Maybe we could—" She broke off suddenly, stood very still. The thought had hit her with such unexpected force that it took her breath away for a second, left her mouth hanging open.

"Could *what?*" Thimble was untying the sweater she had draped around her waist, shoving it under Cowboy's fist. "Come on—we ain't got all day!"

The turquoise turrets of the hot-dog palace were just visible in the distance. Clare pointed to them. "Maybe we *could* fly," she said.

The old man was standing at the grill, wreathed in smoke. He didn't look up as Clare came bursting through the front door; it was Santiago who saw her first.

"I have to talk to Mr. Morgan," she muttered as she passed him, making a beeline to A.J.'s corner of the kitchen. Santiago said nothing, just left his customer at the cash register and hurried over to his boss to warn him.

"Miss Caldwell?" The old man raised his eyes and did the last thing Clare expected him to do: he smiled. "Oh, miss—well, isn't this—I'm so glad to see you!"

But there was no time for small talk, not with Cowboy's blood leaking out of him faster every second. "Mr. Morgan, please, could you come outside? Downstairs, I mean, in the vacant lot. It's an emergency."

The smile vanished. "Of course," he said.

He left the grill to Santiago, hustled around the counter, wiping his hands on his apron. Clare was already on her way back out the door; he followed her onto the boardwalk, down the rickety wooden stairs that led to the lot where the others were huddled around Cowboy, who was half-sitting, half-lying, leaning up against the building. "What's happened, miss?" A.J. asked. "What's wrong?"

She took a deep breath. "It's my friend, Mr. Morgan. He got hurt. We didn't have anyplace else to go."

A.J. bent over Cowboy, who opened his eyes for a moment, shook his head. "I'm all right," he said. "Just need to rest a minute, that's all." There was blood trickling from the corner of his mouth, blood on his hands; Thimble's sweater was saturated with it already.

"Good God," said A.J. "How did this happen?"

"It don't matter now," said Clare. "Please, you got to help him. There ain't nobody else left, nobody we can trust."

A.J. looked alarmed. "Miss—this boy should be in a hospital. I'll call an ambulance." He started back toward the stairs, but Clare followed him, grabbed his arm. "No, sir, he can't go to the hospital, not any of the ones around here. They'd call that—that Griffey. You don't know him, Mr. Morgan. He ain't what you think. He's hurt Cowboy before. Cowboy'd die before he'd let him near him again."

"What do you mean, miss? *How* did he hurt him? He didn't do *this*?"

Clare waved her hands in frustration. "Not *this*—I don't know how, exactly. Cowboy's the one who could tell you,

209

only he can't talk now. But it's the truth, Mr. Morgan; you got to believe me. Please, sir, you got to help him. Cowboy thought he could take care of everybody by himself, but he got hurt, don't you see? Damn hyenas finally got to him—" She was choking back tears now, making no sense.

"I don't understand, Miss Caldwell. I'm not a doctor—how can I help?"

She wiped her eyes, tried again. "The plane—you could get us out in that, couldn't you? Off the island, I mean? Take us somewhere, anywhere—Philadelphia maybe. That ain't far, but it's a whole other state; Griffey couldn't get to him over there. . . . They'll be watching all the bridges for cars, but if we were on the plane, we'd be okay. We'd be safe, don't you see? You could do it, couldn't you, Mr. Morgan? You'll help him, won't you?"

The old man didn't answer right away. His face was a road map of worry lines; Clare could practically hear the wheels whirring inside his head as he tried desperately to take in the situation, to come to some decision. . . .

"Please, sir," she said, "you gotta help him. If it was Joey, you know you'd do it."

Still A.J. said nothing. But he looked as if he had been kicked in the gut.

Thimble broke away from the others. "There ain't no time to think about it, mister. He'll die if we wait."

The old man looked from one girl to the other. Then he walked back to Cowboy, bent over him again.

Cowboy's eyes fluttered open. "Watch out," he said, shaking his head at A.J. "One slipup and you're gone, man."

"Take it easy, son," said A.J. "Everything's going to be all right."

□ □ □

Clare and the others stayed with Cowboy while A. J. went back inside; the door could only be opened from the basement.

"What if he calls the cops?" Thimble asked anxiously. "Are you sure you can trust him?"

"I ain't sure of anything," said Clare. "But we gotta trust somebody."

And then the magic wall was opening once more, and there were the old man and Santiago, bringing out the silver plane; it was shining so brightly in the sun that it might have been a miniature sun itself. And even in the midst of their trouble, when the kids saw it coming their faces lit up. *Good Lord, it's beautiful,* Clare thought, wondering that she had never really noticed before. *Now, if only it* works—

If wishes were horses, Mama whispered inside her head. But Clare didn't have time for that trash, not today. . . .

"Come on, Cowboy," she said to him, as she and Thimble and the others tried to get him to his feet. "Gonna take us a ride."

But the old man took over now. "Here, we've got him," he said, and he and Santiago lifted Cowboy as gently as if he had been made of spun glass and carried him to the plane's first set of passenger seats. They strapped him in between the two girls, then put the other boys in back, with Shoe in the middle. Up on the boardwalk a small crowd had gathered, pointing and talking excitedly, but Clare and the others paid them no mind.

"Where's Racer?" Cowboy mumbled. "We gotta get Racer."

"It's okay," Clare told him. "You already got him, remember? He's right behind us."

211

"Sure, man," said Racer, brushing his streaming eyes roughly with the back of his hand. "I'm right here, Cowboy. I ain't gonna screw up no more, don't worry."

And now the old man was climbing in the cockpit, signaling Santiago to give the propeller a spin while he cranked up the engine—

Pucketa-pucketa-pucketa-phrummm! it roared, starting on the very first try, and Cowboy's eyes flew open again.

"What's that?" he worried. "Watch out, you guys."

"It's just the plane," said Clare. "Don't be afraid."

"He ain't afraid," Thimble snapped. "You ain't afraid of nothing, are you, Cowboy?"

"Not of flying," he said. "Just of crashing." And he closed his eyes again, smiling a little at his own joke.

"Hold on!" the old man called over his shoulder. "Here we go!"

And then the plane was moving across the hard-packed sand of the vacant lot, moving out slowly at first, toward the west. It turned around at the far end, hesitated there for a moment, while the engine grew louder still—

Pucketa-pucketa-PHHHHRRRRRRUUUUMMMMM!

And now they were really moving; the plane was running fast and smooth like a kid in a joyful game of tag, tearing headlong toward the flimsy plywood wall that separated the lot from the underpinnings of the boardwalk. And just when Clare thought they were going to hit it for sure, the silver bird *lifted* off the earth with a mighty bound, leaving her stomach somewhere far below—

"Oh!" she gasped. "We're in the air, Cowboy! Can you feel it? We're flying!"

"Flying," he repeated, but his eyes were closed tight

against the pain, and his face was the color of unwashed sheets, except for the bright flag of red at his lips.

"Hurry!" Thimble shouted at the old man. "You got to hurry!"

"He's hurrying," Clare told her. "Look, Cowboy—it's great! Feel the wind? I ain't never been in an aeroplane before, have you? Looks like we're flying straight into the sun—can't hardly turn your eyes that way for the sparkle. And there's the water under us—you gotta see it shining, Cowboy! I never saw anything so blue, did you? And all those toy boats and little tiny people—they're waving at us, see there? They're wishing us luck—"

"Shoe's sick," said Cowboy, shaking his head. There was a strange little gurgling sound in his voice. "He needs a doctor."

"We're taking him to a doctor, Cowboy. We're taking you both—"

"Hurry!" Thimble shouted at A.J. again. "Can't this thing go any faster?"

"He's *hurrying!*" Clare shouted back. "We're turning, see there?"

It was true; suddenly the sky was tilting toward the sea, or the sea toward the sky, Clare couldn't have said which, and the whole of Atlantic City was sweeping beneath them—looking better than it had ever even thought about looking up close. "Come on, Cowboy," she pleaded now, "open your eyes. You don't want to miss this! You can see everything: there's the playground over there and Atlantic Jack's and the Super-Loops going around right this minute, and there's Ocean One and the Taj Mahal—looks like the circus, don't it? Come on, Cowboy, it's great. Please open your eyes!"

213

And he did; he opened them, but he wasn't seeing what the others were seeing. "Did somebody feed the dog?" he asked. "I can't remember everything—"

"Stop it!" Thimble said fiercely, giving his shoulders a shake. "Don't talk crazy! That's what they do in all those old war movies—those baby-faced guys named Lucky or Nebraska or whatever—the ones you know are dead before they ever fire a shot. You ain't gonna do that to us, Cowboy, do you hear me? Don't you dare die, you jerk!"

"What's wrong?" Little Dog hollered up from the backseat. "Is he worse?"

"He's fine!" Clare lied, yelling back into the three frightened faces. "He's doing just fine!"

"They put him to sleep," Cowboy said quite clearly. "I forgot."

"Put who to sleep, Cowboy?" Clare asked. "You talking about that old dog again?"

"He bit that kid who teased him, remember? So they put him to sleep. I hated that kid."

"Forget the dog, Cowboy. That's history, man. Just like Atlantic City—see there, we're past the island already. It's all behind us now. Ain't nothing ahead but blue sky—d'jya ever see such a blue sky? Look at us, right up here with the birds! We made it, Cowboy; we got away! Old Griffey can't touch us now. . . ."

"Can't touch us," he repeated softly. His eyes were closing again.

"How's he doing?" A.J. called back from the cockpit.

"Just hurry, will you?" Thimble answered. "How much farther do we have to go?"

"Not too far," the old man shouted. "I'm heading over

to Wings Field in Norristown. The radio tower says they'll have an ambulance waiting."

"Hear that, Cowboy? It's gonna be all right. Just a little bit farther."

But Cowboy was mumbling something else now; Clare couldn't quite make it out. "What?" she asked, putting her ear close to his lips; she could feel his hot breath coming fast and shallow, tickling her temple. "What did you say, Cowboy?"

"It wasn't my fault," he whispered hoarsely; there was that odd gurgle in his voice again.

" 'Course not, 'course it wasn't," she assured him, her throat thick with tears. "You did the best you could, better'n anybody else woulda done."

"You guys go on. I'll meet you at the hideout. I just need to rest here for a minute—"

"No!" Clare shouted. "We ain't going anywhere without you, you got that? We stick together—that's the rule. Do you hear me, Cowboy? Looka here now. We're almost there—see the river up ahead? It's the Delaware, ain't it, Cowboy! We're crossing the Delaware same as old George Washington, ain't that great? Ain't that something, Cowboy?"

But Cowboy didn't answer.

25

"HE'S DEAD," said Racer. "I know he's dead."

"Shut up, Racer." Thimble took a drag off the cigarette she had bummed from a guy on the elevator, ground it to pieces on the hospital floor. There were no ashtrays in the waiting room. "The paramedics got his heart started again, remember? He ain't dead."

Racer wiped his eyes on his sleeve. "That don't mean nothing. I seen this before. They charge 'em up with that electric juice, hook 'em to them machines that keep 'em ticking awhile, that's all. Don't mean squat if they don't wake up."

"He'll wake up," said Little Dog, frowning at his own two fists, clenched in his lap. "They said it was lucky they got to him when they did."

Racer shook his head. "Naw, man, I seen his face. Looked just like my cousin's when—looked just like him. Oh, he's dead, all right."

"*Shut up, Racer.*" Thimble's voice was dangerous. "He ain't dead, you got that?"

Racer closed his mouth, sat sniffling quietly, pulling at a small rip in the vinyl of his armrest.

"Don't worry," Clare told him, giving his shoulder an encouraging shake. "He's gonna be okay. It's *Cowboy*, remember?"

"I don't know, Hatso." Racer kept his voice low, so as not to get Thimble riled again. "He looked bad, man."

Clare had no other answer. She was trying to shut out the terrible image that kept flashing before her: Cowboy's torn body lying on that stretcher, still as the grave, tubes coming out of him every which way. Blood all over the place—on the sheets, on the paramedics' white coats and plastic-wrapped hands, on Thimble and Clare—everywhere but in Cowboy, where it belonged. And his eyes, she kept seeing those, too—the brown eyes only half-covered by the lids, staring at who knew what? That skeleton in the black robe, maybe. . . .

Clare shivered, tried to push the thought away. She picked up an ancient issue of *Sports Illustrated* from the chair next to her, looked at it for a while, though the words made no sense to her and her tears kept smudging the pictures, falling in great wet splats on batting helmets and belly buttons alike. They had been here for hours now, waiting in the waiting room, while Cowboy clung to life in the trauma unit down the hall and Shoe fought his own battle upstairs in the children's ward. The doctor in the emergency room had taken one look at him and had him whisked away, too.

"They ought to let me stay with him," Racer had worried. "They ain't gonna know how to ask him stuff. They ain't gonna understand about him."

217

"It'll be all right, son," A.J. had assured him. "They just want him to rest now. They've given him something to help him sleep. But I'll have them call you the minute there's anything you can do."

The old man had been in and out of the waiting room all afternoon, bringing news of the patients, food and drink for the others, and all the encouragement he knew how to give—though he looked so worried himself that you could hardly call him a ray of sunshine. Still, it was good to have him there, good to have *somebody* in their corner, even if it was just one peculiar old man. . . .

He came in again now and was immediately surrounded.

"Any change? Any news?" four voices asked at once.

"Well," he began, making an attempt at a smile, "your younger friend—ah, Shoe?—seems to be doing a little better. The doctors were worried about dehydration, but they believe they've caught it in time. He's sleeping now. They say you'll be able to see him in the morning."

"And Cowboy?" Thimble asked anxiously.

A.J. shook his head. "There's no change so far. But they're doing everything they can. He's got youth on his side; that means so much, you know. . . ." He hesitated. "It's just that he's lost a lot of blood."

Little Dog's eyes widened suddenly. "Couldn't we—isn't there a way we could give him some of *our* blood?" he asked eagerly. "For transfusions, I mean?"

"Yeah!" the others cried together. "We could do that!" and "That's a great idea!" and "Sure, man; I got plenty—he can have all he wants!"

But A.J. shook his head again. "They say there are age limits. Seventeen to sixty-five."

He had already asked, then; he had already offered his own blood. "We're too young and you're too old," Clare murmured. She hated needles, but she would gladly have faced a whole truckload of them if it would have helped Cowboy; any one of them would have. It didn't seem fair— that they couldn't even give him this one little piece of themselves.

"So there's nothing we can do." Thimble's voice was bitter.

"Well," the old man said quietly, "we can pray."

Right, thought Clare. *Fat lot of good that's gonna do.*

And he must have seen it in her eyes, because he colored and added quickly, "Of course, I don't know how you feel about that sort of thing." His smile was apologetic. "But it couldn't hurt."

Day slogged along at a snail's pace, becoming night at last, and still there was no change, no change. . . . A.J. offered to take Clare and the others to a motel so they could get some sleep, but they refused; no way would they leave their friends.

It was late when he returned again—no change, he told them—but he needed to speak to Miss Caldwell alone. . . .

"There have been some questions," he said in a low voice. They were standing in the hall now, out of earshot of the others.

Clare's heart sank. "Questions? What kind of questions? Who's asking questions?"

"Only the hospital staff, so far. But when there's a knife wound, the police are automatically notified. And since we're from Atlantic City—I had to give them my address, you see—it's likely they'll want to get in touch with the authorities there, too."

Griffey, thought Clare. *Good Lord in heaven.* They weren't safe *yet*, then? Even in another state, even on the outskirts of the City of Brotherly Love? He was like the devil himself; no matter how far you ran, he was there before you. . . .

"No," she said. "They can't—"

"I'm afraid they can. They'll want to talk to you—in the morning, I imagine. It's only questions, miss. The people here—they want to help, but they can't do anything if they don't understand. And I don't know enough to explain it to them, don't you see? No one can help unless you tell us what's happened."

"But—it was an accident. We already told you—"

"About the man with the knife—yes, I know. It's the rest of it they want you to clear up—why we had to come here, this trouble with—with Mr. Griffey, you said?"

"They'd say we were lying. Nobody would understand."

The old man smiled gently. "Try me," he said. "I only want to help, Miss Caldwell."

She believed him. *Sometimes people* are *what they seem*. . . . But she could only shake her head helplessly. How could *she* explain? Cowboy was the one who had to tell them about Griffey, and he was in no shape now, was he? He wouldn't be coming to the rescue this time. This time they were on their own. But there was nothing they could do. . . .

"What did he want?" Thimble asked, joining Clare in the hall when the old man had left again to check on Cowboy and Shoe.

"He don't know what to tell the hospital people," Clare explained. "He says they have to call the police in Atlantic City, because they don't understand about—" She broke off suddenly. She had almost forgotten; this morning was ancient history—all of them huddling under the tarp in the gardener's truck, Thimble asking Cowboy if Griffey was going there for Racer—

"About what?" Thimble asked now.

"About Griffey."

Thimble didn't say anything for a moment. Her face showed nothing. "Oh," she said at last, then turned to go back inside.

But Clare grabbed her arm. "*You* know about him, don't you? You could tell them."

Thimble shook loose. "You don't know what you're talking about," she muttered. "You don't know anything about it."

"Yes, I do. Cowboy told me."

Thimble looked at her in disbelief. "He told *you*?"

"Not all of it. But some. Enough."

Thimble was still wordless, so Clare rushed on, "He hurt you, too, didn't he, Thimble? And Cowboy found out about it. Cowboy got you away somehow."

"That's nobody's business."

"Yes, it is. You know it is. It's Cowboy's business, for starters. It's Racer's business if the cops say he has to go back. It's everybody's business—any kid who comes around looking for help and Griffey's what they find."

"They'd never believe me."

"A.J. would. And the others—well, if they don't, we ain't no worse off than we are right now, are we? At least you'll know you tried to stop him. At least you'll know you put up a fight."

Thimble didn't answer, so Clare tried again. "If you don't, he wins, don't you get it? If we run away again, he

221

wins. He thinks he's won already—you saw him. He's so sure of himself, he thinks nobody has the nerve to do anything about him. He thinks he can walk right up to you in front of God and everybody and you ain't gonna do a thing about it. Don't that make you *sick*, Thimble?"

"Sure it makes me sick," she growled. "Plenty of things make me sick."

"So fight him. Fight for Cowboy. It was Griffey who stabbed him, same as if he held the knife in his hand."

Thimble hesitated again. Clare could see her struggling. But then she shook her head. "It's easy for you to talk. You don't know what it would be like. You don't know how it feels."

Clare didn't answer right away. The red was creeping up her neck. "Yes, I do," she said at last.

Thimble grew quiet. "Griffey?" she said, after a moment.

"No." It was washing over her again—that wave of revulsion. She had to lean against the wall to keep from sinking. "Not Griffey. Cowboy warned me about him. It was someone else, before I came here."

Another silence. And then Thimble said, "And did you—did you ever tell anybody about *him*?"

Clare looked at her sneakers. They were getting pretty worn out now; the summer had taken its toll. . . . She took a deep breath, let it out slowly. "No," she said. "I never did."

Thimble just stared at her for a minute. Then she went back into the waiting room, sat down. She didn't have to say it; she didn't have to say, "So how can you tell me what *I* have to do?" The words were already thick in the air between them.

□   □   □

Clare slipped off by herself after a while, pretending she needed to go to the bathroom. No telling what the others would have thought if they had seen her coming in here, into this dim little wood-and-glass box of a chapel. Empty, at this late hour. Clare slid into the very last pew. There were just a half dozen of them, facing a large picture window, dark now. A plain white cross hung before it from the ceiling, just above the altar, which was covered with a cloth on which somebody had embroidered the words "God Is Love." A handful of mismatched floral arrangements were propped up around it—probably left over from patients who had already gone home. *Or died*, thought Clare, trying not to look at the drooping lilies, the chrysanthemums with their petals just beginning to flake.

She sat there for a while, feeling like a fool, unsure how to begin. It had been so long; she was out of practice. And even if she had known all the right words, even if there really was a God Who could hear her, she had broken so many of His rules since Nashville that she doubted they were on speaking terms anymore. Still, A.J. was right; it couldn't hurt, could it? Who knew, maybe the Almighty would cut a deal—

Okay, look, she prayed, *I'll do anything You want. I'll never steal another penny. I'll be clean as a nun. Shoot, I'll be a nun, if only You'll let Cowboy be all right, if only You'll get us out of this mess.*

God doesn't make deals, she could hear Father Cavanaugh saying. *It doesn't work that way.*

So how does it work? Could somebody please tell me that?

223

There was no answer. Unless you counted those words leering at her from the altar like some cheesy bumper sticker:

GOD IS LOVE

Love. What a joke. What a big fat freaking gyp. Oh, sure, she knew about love; she was a bloody expert on the subject. There was nothing nice about it, nothing pretty like in the movies. It was a mess, was what it was. She hurt all over from it. It was as if somebody had ripped her open and her insides were spilling out like Cowboy's—worse than just an aching heart: aching head, aching ears, aching teeth, liver, big toe, and appendix. There was love gushing from holes in her arms and legs and belly—love for all of them, none of them. Here was a little rip for her real daddy—hardly more than a pinprick, that one; she didn't remember him enough for it to hurt as much as the rest, nowhere near the stab wound Joey Morgan had left. And the others were even worse: Cowboy—oh, God, yes, Cowboy—and Racer with his cocksure grin and Shoe the silent air-eater and Little Dog, notebook and all, and even—well, maybe it wasn't love pouring out of the hole Thimble had made but it stung anyway, whatever it was. Respect maybe; that was more like it. Nothing she couldn't bear, nothing to the gash for Jessie James. Oh, yes, Clare loved her still, Lord help her, even when she hated her so. Oh, Mama, that still hurt the most of all, didn't it? Didn't it? Or maybe love and hate weren't big enough words for all the confusing things she felt for Mama—lovehatefeardisgustpitypridesorrow*anger*, that was what she felt for her mother and oh, how it hurt, it hurt, it was killing her, this feeling, this mixed-up yearn-

224

inganguish. Only Griffey did she hate with a pure uncomplicated hatred; only Sid did she hate without limit.

They're the bad guys, Mama; they're the ones who did wrong. Not me, Mama, not me. . . .

You have to spit it out, sister. You have to say the words.

I can't—

Yes, you can. If you don't, they win. If you run away again, they win.

How could I say it, Mama? How could I ever tell you how it was—that night when you were passed out cold and he came into my room while I was asleep and the next thing I knew I could hardly breathe: his hand was over my mouth and I was afraid, Mama; I couldn't move I was so afraid. . . . Why didn't you stop him? Why didn't you come? How could you sleep through my tears, Mama?

And she wept again now; she buried her face in her arms and she sobbed as if her heart would break; she cried out her love and her hate and her fear until there weren't any tears left in her, no tears left in the whole world. She had used them all up; she had cried away lakes and rivers and salty oceans. And at last she grew quieter; she wiped her face with the tail of her blouse, which was really too filthy now to qualify as dork material, and then she sat and stared at the wilted flowers. And after some more time had passed, the door at the back of the chapel opened, and Thimble came in and sat beside her, not looking at her, just studying her own hands. "I'll do it," Thimble said at last. "I'll tell 'em about Griffey. They ain't gonna want to hear it, but I'll tell 'em."

And that was all, until finally Little Dog and Racer came in, too, and lay down on the smooth wooden bench beside the girls. And eventually they slept, all but Clare; at first every now and then one of them would make a little hiccuping, gasping noise, as if an unspent sob were trying to escape. But after a while even that stopped, and there was no sound in the room, only Clare's blood thrumming in her ears. For once even the voices in her head were quiet; there was no need for their arguing anymore. She knew what she had to do.

She didn't know what time it was when the picture window began to glow with a pale gray light. There was just the barest hint of dawn at first and then the real thing, streaking the east with long purple fingers like the ones Clare used to smear across her art paper in kindergarten. She could see the trees now, a stand of young maples that were just beginning to turn, splotched with yellow and orange and red, the color of Cowboy's blood. Tossing in the morning breeze, bright against the blueing sky.

Come on, God, she prayed, *maybe You don't do deals, but they say You ain't bad at miracles. What's one little miracle, more or less?*

She must have slept, too, then, because the next thing she knew the old man was beside her, giving her shoulder a gentle shake. "I'm sorry to wake you, miss, but—please wake up, Miss Caldwell."

She bolted upright, awake at once.

There were tears in A.J.'s eyes.

"What is it?" she asked. "Is Cowboy—is he . . . ?" She couldn't bring herself to say the word.

But Racer said it for her: "He's dead, ain't he? Cowboy's dead."

They were all awake now, looking at the old man. He cleared his throat; he seemed to be having trouble with his voice. "No," he managed at last, "no, he's better." A.J. was shaking his head now, smiling through his tears. "The doctors think the worst is over. He's asking for you. For all of you."

26

IT WAS a wonder they didn't kill somebody, the way they tore out of the chapel, hurtling past a pair of startled orderlies, nearly flattening a nurse's aide carrying a loaded breakfast tray, barely avoiding a collision with a girl on crutches. Cries of "Hey!" and "What in the—" and "That's not allowed in here!" followed them, but they didn't—couldn't—slow down, not until they arrived, panting, at Cowboy's door.

"Just for a few minutes," the nurse warned them, putting a finger to her lips. "He's still awfully weak." But she was smiling, too.

He did look weak; he looked pretty terrible, to tell the truth, still stuck up with tubes and gray as skim milk, his black curls plastered damply to his forehead. But at least the brown eyes were open; at least they were really *seeing* now, looking out at his friends as they eased up cautiously around his bed.

"Hey, guys," he said—in almost his regular voice. "That was some trip, huh?"

"You said it, man," Racer managed to choke out, grinning. "Better'n the Super-Loops."

Thimble looked fierce. "You ain't gonna start in on that old *dog* again, are you?" she growled.

"Dog?" Cowboy seemed puzzled. "What dog?"

"Never mind," she said, taking a tissue from the box by his bed and giving her nose a good blow.

"How's Shoe?" he asked.

"He's doing okay," said Little Dog. "They said we could see him in a little while."

"Great." Cowboy smiled a little, then closed his eyes. He was exhausted already, it seemed. "Turned out all right, then, didn't it? We got away. . . ."

Not quite, Clare thought. *Not yet.* She looked at Thimble, who gave her a small nod in return. *But we're going to.*

They went to A.J. first.

"We can trust him," Clare told Thimble. "He proved it, didn't he?"

He seemed fairly calm about it in the beginning, though Clare noticed the flames in his cheeks when he and Thimble finished talking. But then she had expected that. And he was quiet during the opening of the session with the two police officers who arrived a little later to ask their questions. But when Griffey's name came up at last, when Thimble was struggling to explain what sort of man he was, and the officers looked at each other and one of them said he hoped Thimble realized the seriousness of the charges she was making against a respected member of the community, A.J. leapt to his feet.

229

"Respected member of—the fellow ought to be strung up!" he exploded. "These children—do you have any idea what they've been through? Any *idea*? The boy might have *died*, do *you* realize *that*, sir?"

"Calm down, Mr. Morgan," the officer answered. "Just take it easy."

"Take it *easy*? When monsters like that are allowed to walk the streets? What are we thinking of? Take it *easy*? They didn't have anywhere to turn, don't you see that? Who's looking out for these children while we're *taking it easy*, will somebody tell me that?"

Watching him, Clare felt like laughing and crying and cheering all at once. He hadn't had enough practice at being mad; he wasn't very *good* at it, really. The veins stuck out in his neck, he turned a new shade of red every five seconds, and he was trembling—actually *trembling* with rage. But it didn't matter; all that mattered was that he believed them, that he was on their side. . . .

For a while it looked as if A.J. might be the only one. Even when Cowboy was well enough to be told what was happening, even when he came forward to back up Thimble's story—no way was he going to let her take the heat all alone—Griffey just went straight to the press and denied every word. Suddenly the newspapers and TV screens were full of his smiling face. Only it wasn't smiling so much now; it was looking all injured and pious. Cowboy and Thimble were "troubled," he said; he felt nothing but "compassion" for them. He had tried to help them, but they were "beyond help"—compulsive liars and thieves, both of them; their records spoke for themselves. And now they were making these terrible accusations out of jealousy or greed or just

230

plain orneriness—who knew? It was "very sad"; that was all he could say.

"What a jerk," said Thimble, throwing the paper she'd been reading into the trash can. "And he thinks *we're* sad!"

"How can he do it?" Clare asked. "How can he say those things with a straight face?"

Cowboy shook his head. "He makes himself believe it. That's how the best liars work. He remembers whatever it suits him to remember."

"Sounds like a pretty good trick," Thimble growled. "If you can pull it off."

"He *won't* pull it off." Cowboy's voice was gruff. "Not this time. We're not gonna let him."

"At least the agency fired him, right?" Clare asked. "At least he ain't gonna bother anybody else."

"It's a leave of absence, that's all," said Cowboy. "Just until the investigation's over. A.J. says these things can take a while."

It ain't fair, Clare thought. Seemed as if the only way the kids could fight back was to tear themselves apart, cracking the gang into so many pieces that it was like old Humpty Dumpty; no way it would ever be the same again. But it was too late to run from the devil; they had chosen to stick around and slug it out.

And so they went back to Atlantic City with A.J., back to the hot-dog palace, at first: Clare and Racer and Thimble and Little Dog and—when he was up to it—Cowboy, too. All but Shoe. He had grinned quietly the day they finally brought him down to see Cowboy, but he was drained; anybody could see that—worn clear through to the nub like Clare's old sneakers. The doctors tried to explain that he was sicker than any of them had understood before—hurting

231

in more than just his poor little body. For now they were moving him to another hospital—this one especially for children—a place that would really know how to help him begin to heal, they said. . . .

"What if it's just like that other one?" Racer worried. "Only this time I won't be there to look out for him."

"He'll be all right," Cowboy promised, so forcefully that Clare knew he was trying to make himself believe it, too. "A.J. says the doctors there are supposed to be really great with kids like Shoe. They might even be able to get him to talk again. I bet next time we see him, he'll be cracking wiser than you."

Racer wiped his eyes on his sleeve, brightened a little at that thought. "That'd be something, wouldn't it? Old Shoe—a regular comedian—turning up on Letterman or something. Telling stories about the old days on the boardwalk, maybe. Think he'll talk about me and him and Frank?" And he gave Shoe his tiny plastic sword as a going-away present, just so he'd remember. . . .

Racer himself was going with Little Dog to a group home on a farm near Lumberton. "I guess I'll try it for a *while*," he told Clare, shaking his head doubtfully, the day she and Cowboy and Thimble saw the two of them off at the bus station. "But I don't know how long I can last. I mean, can you see me in the country, man? With *chickens* and crud?"

Little Dog looked pretty torn up about it, too. "It'll be okay," he said, trying to smile as he tucked his notebook in his back pocket. "It's free, right?"

"It's just for a little while," Cowboy swore. He and Thimble were staying with two different foster families in

Ventnor for now. "Just until Shoe's better and this mess with Griffey is over. Then we'll come for you. I promise."

Thimble didn't say much, just hugged the two boys fiercely and muttered, "Hang tough, you guys." And then they shook hands with Cowboy and Clare and climbed on the bus, and when they found their seats, they waved from the window, and Racer hiked it up and hollered, "Bye, Cowboy! See ya later, Hatso!"

Clare waved back, but she couldn't find her voice, couldn't make a sound as she stood there between Cowboy and Thimble, watching the bus pull out. She wondered if she really would see them later—if she would ever see them again. The thought made her hurt all over.

She would be leaving, too, before long, trying for that fresh start that Mama kept talking about. Going home. It hadn't been easy, living up to the promise she had made to herself that dark night in the hospital chapel. It had taken every bit of her courage, picking up the phone, dialing the number, listening to the faraway ringing. Even then at the last second she had come within a hairsbreadth of chickening out, hanging up before the second ring. But she had gritted her teeth, held on to the receiver for dear life . . . and at last there had been the answering click, the sound of Jessie's voice—

"Hello?"

"Hey, Mama. It's me."

They had talked for nearly an hour that first day. Talked and talked and talked some more. And Mama had told her how she was going to change, how she was trying already—getting help with her drinking problem, joining a group that was especially for people like her. And then Clare had taken a deep breath and said, "That's great, Mama. That's really great. But the drinking—it wasn't the only reason I left."

"What do you mean, sister? What else was there?"

And Clare had done it; she had spit it all out—one word first and then another and another. And Mama had believed her. She had cried like a baby, and to her credit she had done more than that; she had shown the bum the door that very day—that very hour. She had even called the cops and tried to prosecute, but Sid skipped town before they could catch him. Clare suspected he wasn't so much afraid of the police as he was of Jessie James.

The crazy thing was that even though all this time Clare had thought she wanted to go home, if only *he* was gone, now that she really had the chance, she was having second thoughts. The whole deal smacked a little too much of the ruby slippers—click your heels and think of Kansas and presto! There's no place like home. Although she doubted Auntie Em drank much, and nobody had ever accused Uncle What's-His-Name of being a lech. . . .

It was scary trusting Mama again, that was all. Nobody was forcing her; Jessie had agreed to let her stay on at A.J.'s for the time being, while she tried to prove she really meant it about cleaning up her act in Nashville. And meanwhile Clare was sitting pretty in her tower room, with A.J. looking after her. Even Santiago seemed to like her a little better now; he had baked her a chocolate pie on her birthday without saying a word about the one she had stolen, just smiled and told A.J. he had a feeling it was Miss Caldwell's favorite. (That was a first—a birthday pie. Almost took the ache out of turning thirteen in New Jersey.) And the cast was gone and her hair was nearly grown out and all that was left of the old eggplant was a neat little half of a railroad-track scar just above her right eyebrow, and her bangs covered that pretty well; the pageant officials didn't have to start polishing the crown yet, but at least babies didn't cry when they saw her coming. She had even been going to eighth grade at the local school and liked it some—

Which was why it was terrifying—the idea of risking everything, trying again with Mama. A person could get *hurt*. . . . But then sometimes at night it would come back—that deep-down wordless wanting. And there was no arguing with it.

So in spite of all her doubts, two weeks before Christmas she went shopping with A.J. for a new travel bag. They bought it at O'Farrell's in the luggage department, just across the aisle from the ladies' shoes. Clare looked for Miss Montana, but she was nowhere to be seen; could be she had won the prize for congeniality and was already out making dental-floss commercials. In her place was a sour-looking man with a thin black mustache who was frowning at an undecided customer. Clare couldn't help thinking how differently everything might have turned out if it had been *his* shift that day she had come here with Thimble. . . .

They picked out a nice gray bag with a sturdy-looking zipper and extra pockets.

"Are you *sure*, miss?" A.J. must have asked her a dozen times. "Are you absolutely certain?"

Clare knew it wasn't just the bag he was worrying about. "Yes, sir," she said, trying her best to believe it. "Thank you, sir. I'll pay you back someday."

A.J. blushed. "Oh, no, miss, it's—well, it's a Christmas present, that's all."

"But—I don't have—"

"No, no, please . . . I'll tell you what you can do. Just

235

drop me a letter from time to time, will you? Let me know how you're getting along?"

"Well, sure, but—"

"I promise to answer," he added quietly.

Santiago was on the kitchen phone when they got back. "No," he was saying, "she's not—" and then he looked up and saw Clare and A.J., and he waved to her and said into the phone, "Excuse me. She's just walking in the door."

He held out the receiver, and she picked it up and said, "Mama?" They spoke on the phone a couple of times a week now. . . .

But it wasn't Jessie.

"Hey, kiddo," said Joey Morgan. "How's it going?"

It took a few seconds for Clare to get control of her tongue. It had swollen suddenly, become a useless lump lolling about in her mouth. "Joey?" she said at last—so weakly that she had to clear her throat and try again. "Joey—is that you?"

"It's me," he said. "The old pinhead himself." She could hear him chuckling three thousand miles away; wasn't that amazing? Or was he . . . ?

"Are you—are you still in California?"

"Yes, ma'am. Well, I'm here *now*; I had a road gig for a few months—just got back a couple of days ago. So I was going through a pile of mail that my—my friend's been saving for me, and there were your letters—yours and Pop's."

"Oh," said Clare. So that was it. All those months of waiting, all those gallons of tears, explained away in a couple of breaths.

"So what's up, kiddo? Are you all right now? Pop said

in his letter that you'd had—some kind of accident. You didn't mention it."

"Oh, well, it wasn't any big deal. I just—just tripped, that's all. I'm fine now," she said, glad he couldn't see her blushing.

"Well, that's great. That's just great, then. He had me kind of worried. But I'm glad everything's okay now. . . ." Joey had a little coughing fit then; probably still smoking too much, she worried. "So anyway, kiddo," he continued, when he had got his breath back, "what's all this about you coming out here? You, uh, you and Jess—your mom— you guys had a little run-in, I guess?"

Now even the tips of her ears were burning. "Yeah, well," she stammered, "something—something like that." A *little run-in?* Was that all it was?

"I'm sorry to hear that, Clare. I'm really sorry, honey. Not much of a summer vacation, huh, kiddo?"

"Well," Clare began, "it—" And then she paused, struck by a sudden vision: Racer turning on the "Magic Fingers" in the motel room, Thimble shrieking, Shoe giggling, Little Dog doling out pizza with olives. And Cowboy's brown eyes sparking laughter as he leaned across a table lit with fat purple candles and handed her a small silver hat. . . .

Clare leaned her forehead against the glass covering the bee-bearded man: He Is Only Rich, Who Owns the Day. "Oh, well," she murmured, "it had its moments."

There was an awkward pause, and then Joey said, "So anyway, about this California deal—I guess things have changed now, right? Since you wrote your letter?"

"Well—sure, a lot of stuff's happened since then, but—"

"I mean, you sounded pretty desperate, kiddo. And if you still *needed* a place to stay, well, we'd just work something out, you know? If you were still in—some kind of trouble, I mean. . . . But now—"

He didn't finish the sentence.

"We?" Clare asked. "Who's we?"

"Well, Melissa and I. Melissa Gill. Oh, you'd like her. I know you would. She's a singer, like—well, you know, a really terrific singer."

"Oh," said Clare. She had the peculiar sensation of having swallowed a piece of ice whole. "So—so you're living with her now?"

Another pause—Joey taking a deep breath maybe. And then he said, "Yeah, well, sort of, you know. We're just sharing an apartment." *Right. Mr. Commitment.* She had almost forgotten. . . . He was quiet a moment more, and then when Clare didn't say anything, he went on, "It's just a little place—a studio apartment in West Hollywood, you know? You wouldn't believe the rent in this town, kiddo. Nothing like Nashville. Out here you pay through the nose for a cardboard box and a mailing address, know what I mean?"

He paused yet again. *Am I supposed to laugh?* she wondered. "So—so you don't want me to come?" she asked finally.

"Oh, honey, it's not that. We'd both love to have you, if you really need—I mean, you just say the word, that's all, and we'll start trying to figure it out. We'll get you here in time for Christmas, if that's what you really want."

Just say the word. . . .

Clare thought of her latest conversation with Mama—

how excited she had been, talking about buying the Christmas tree next week when Clare got home, hinting at a present that was already wrapped and waiting. . . . And then she thought of last Christmas—Jessie passed out on the couch before dark and the smell of burnt plastic; Clare had tried to cook the turkey, but she had forgotten to take out that little sack full of gizzards in the middle. . . .

"Kiddo? You still there?"

"Yeah. Yeah, I'm here."

"I thought for a second we had lost our connection. . . . So anyhow, what do you say? I mean, now that you know the setup and all? You're welcome, I really mean that."

Clare swallowed hard. That ice was melting now. "It's okay, Joey," she said. "I mean, I really appreciate it. But I guess—I guess I'll go home. Mama's expecting me."

Clare couldn't hear anything for a moment. But she was fairly certain there was a sigh of relief involved somehow. "Well, if you're sure," Joey said at last. "I mean, as long as you're going to be all right."

"I'll be fine," Clare said.

She was just about to hang up when she noticed A.J. over at the counter, fiddling with the soda wheel, trying his best not to listen in on her side of the conversation, though Clare knew it must be killing him. "Wait a minute, Joey. Don't hang up," she said in a rush. "You want to talk to your dad, don't you?"

A couple of seconds passed.

"Joey?"

"Sure," he said. "Sure thing, kiddo. Put him on, will you?"

And so she did.

□ □ □

Halfway through her second week back in Nashville, Clare was sitting with Mama on the couch in the TV/living room, watching some old lady on the tube trying to explain how to carve raw fish into such cute little designs that your guests might not even notice you never got around to cooking it. And Mama got sick of that before long and started switching channels, when just by chance she came across the nature show that Clare and A.J. had seen last summer.

"Oh," Mama said, sitting down again. "I heard this was good."

Clare was about to say she saw it already, but then she stopped. They were getting along pretty well, so far; if Mama wanted to watch it, well, fine. Clare could always leave the room when the rough stuff started. But a part of her wanted to stay, too, though she didn't quite know why. Maybe it was something like pushing on an old bruise, even when you know it's going to hurt. . . .

She let her mind drift as the narrator started talking. This first part was pretty tame, as she recalled: just the opening shots of the lions and hyenas, the lead-in information about the battle they had been waging for thousands and thousands of years. . . . Clare found herself thinking of Cowboy, of the last time she had seen him, walking on the boardwalk, just a couple of days before she left the island. He had stopped to listen to the crippled woman's music.

Clare didn't recognize the tune. "What's that?" she asked.

"I don't know," said Cowboy. "I never heard it before." He looked at the woman's companion, who shrugged.

"Something new," he explained. "Ain't got no words yet."

They walked on together for a while after that.

"How's the investigation going?" Clare asked.

Cowboy shook his head. He looked tired. "Slow," he said. "Griffey's still sticking to his lies. But they've found some of the other kids now. A few of them have started talking. I don't think he'll ever work at the agency again, anyway."

"It's not enough," said Clare.

"No. Nowhere near enough."

They were quiet for a moment, and then Clare asked, "What'll you do when it's over?"

Cowboy leaned on the railing, stared out at the ocean. "I don't know. These people I'm staying with—they want me to stick around, go to school and all. And A.J.—he says I can have a job, if I want it. . . . But I don't know. I promised the others. . . . Maybe we'll get together again, go down south. Someplace you don't have to worry about the cold in January. Florida maybe. They have boardwalks down there, too."

"Not *the* boardwalk," said Clare. *Oh, Cowboy.* "Not *our* boardwalk."

Cowboy turned to her, held her gently with his eyes. Then he picked up a stray piece of popcorn, threw it to a passing gull that swooped down and caught it in midair. "It was never our boardwalk," he said. "Not really."

Clare focused on the TV screen. Here she was now, that poor doomed lioness, going off to have her kids. Only the snake was there just like before, and the babies died all over again. And Clare ached for her as she got sicker and weaker and stumbled off looking for water—

"The poor thing," Mama murmured, but they kept watching, even though Clare dreaded what was coming next: devil's laughter, it sounded like—snarling, howling, *yip yap yowllli*ng, closing in from the surrounding darkness. And still they watched as the lioness tried desperately to fend off her enemies, fighting them with her last ounce of strength, though she was blind and bleeding and there was no way, no way at all for her to win. . . .

But then a strange thing happened. Just when it seemed as if the lioness's luck had run out altogether, the hyenas began to look confused. All that last-ditch roaring and carrying-on had faked them out somehow, made them think she might be a little tougher than they had bargained on. And so they backed off; doggone if those old pug-ugly cowards didn't turn tail and run. And as time passed, the lioness got better; little by little the poison worked itself out of her system, until finally she was well enough to find her way back to her pride. And they were glad to see her.

For a moment Clare just sat there with her mouth hanging open. And then she got up off the couch and went to her room and started a letter on her Christmas stationery:

Dear Mr. Morgan,
  Good news. . . .